Tales from the Palace of the Fairy King

DANIEL Z. LIEBERMAN

For Zach and Sam, who inspired the stories in this book. They gave encouragement and wise advice. Among many other things, I owe the title of this book to Zach.

I also owe a debt of gratitude to Mike Long, an outstanding writer, an incisive editor, and a good friend.

CONTENTS

THE MAGIC SPYGLASS

P eter Hedley was a farmer who had a large family, a poor farm, and a face that was troubled by thoughts of disaster. Part of Peter's family lived inside a tumble-down farmhouse. He had a wife, three sons, and a young daughter. The other part lived behind the farmhouse. It was a collection of small animals that Peter had rescued. Whenever he saw an animal that had been hurt, or had fallen from its nest, he carried it back to the farmhouse.

Today, a squirrel had cut its leg on the sharp edge of a scythe. It lay on the ground, its fur matted with blood. Peter picked it up, and wrapped it in his shirt. The squirrel trembled in his hands, and Peter knew how it felt.

He put it in one of the cages that were stacked against the back of the farmhouse. Peter built the cages out of scraps of wood and leftover nails. Most of the cages had holes in them, but Peter believed that if an animal crawled through a hole and got away, it was because it was ready to go, so that was all right.

He gave the squirrel some straw to sleep on, and put an apple and an ear of corn in the cage for it to eat.

Peter's daughter, Rose, was the one who named the animals. After dinner she and Peter took their chairs outside, and sat in front of the cages until the stars came out. Peter told Rose everything he knew about the squirrel: what part of the farm it lived in, how he had found it, and what it looked like when he first saw it. Rose squinted her eyes at the squirrel until she understood it inside and out. Then she gave it a name that was just right.

Peter couldn't spend as much time with his animals as he wanted to, because his farm needed so much work. It was on a hard piece of land that was full of stones. The land flooded when it rained, and cracked with drought if the sun shone for more than three days in a row. If Peter had known what a bad piece of land it was, he would have bought a different farm, and he almost did.

As a young man, Peter had saved every penny he could for eight long years, and he worried about finding the right place. It was a relief when a friend told him about a good farm that was for sale. It was owned by a farmer who had grown old, and was going away to live with his son. The farm was just right for Peter, and he was about to buy it, when a man named Jarvis told him to be careful. Jarvis knew a lot about buying and selling land, and he had a reputation for being clever—some said too clever.

"You never know what you're going to get when you buy land," Jarvis had said one day. "You've got to watch out, and stay sharp."

Peter nodded. He knew he was taking an important step, and he worried about it day and night.

"What do you know about buying land, Peter?"

"Not very much. I've worked on a few farms. I've seen some good ones and some bad ones."

"Ah, that makes you an expert, does it?"

"No. I'm not an expert."

"You think because you've worked on farms, you know the business of buying and selling pretty well."

"I don't know anything about it at all."

"Nothing?"

"No."

"Peter, I can see we're headed for trouble. I can see it as plain as day. You're telling me you know nothing about the business—your words, not mine—but in spite of that, you're about to put down your life's savings on a farm that's nothing more nor less than a complete mystery to you."

"It was recommended to me by a friend, and it looks like it's exactly what I need."

"Ah, that's different. You have a friend who's an expert in buying and selling land. Very good, Peter, that makes all the difference in the world."

"Well, he's not an expert, but he knows something about these things, and I trust him."

Peter and Jarvis were walking down a dirt road that led to the village. The sun was out, and the dust made Peter's clothes itch. Now Jarvis stopped, and turned to face Peter.

"My ears must be playing tricks on me, Peter. You tell me your friend is no expert, and then in the same breath you say you trust him with the most important purchase of your life? That's how it is? That's the man I'm dealing with, Peter Hedley? Well, then, I must wish you good day. I'm an honest man, you know that, Peter, and I make it a rule never to do business with a fool. It's a shame, too, because I happen to know of a farm that's bigger, better, and will cost you less money than the one your so-called 'expert' friend wants you to buy.

"But since you've no use for real experts, Peter—people who actually know something about the business—there's a wide-awake young man in town who's been looking for just such a bargain. He's been pestering me about this farm for days, and I might as well call on him tomorrow morning. It's too bad, Peter. This young man's not like you and me. We're the same. We understand each other. To be perfectly honest with you, the young man I speak of doesn't deserve the farm. I'd much rather you had it. It would set you up for life as a rich man. What a shame! Good-bye, Peter."

Jarvis hadn't really walked away, and in the end Peter had bought the farm that Jarvis said would make him a rich man. Jarvis was right about it being bigger than the one his friend had found for him, and it did cost less money, but it didn't make him rich. Quite the opposite; Peter struggled with the hard piece of land, and was barely able to make enough to support his family.

"If only we had more money," he thought, as he lay awake in his bed at night. "Then I wouldn't worry so much. If I were rich, I'd never worry again."

Peter's sons never worried. They just grew bigger and

stronger every year. They liked to help their father on the farm, and they liked to fight with each other even more. His daughter never worried. Her brothers were kind to her, and when they played with her, she had everything in the world she could possibly want. His wife didn't worry, either.

"We always have more than enough to be thankful for. I wish you wouldn't let things bother you so much."

She pressed his frowning face between her cool hands.

"Now smile at me," she said with laughter in her eyes.

Peter smiled, and he felt better. But, still, he wasn't sure about the "always more than enough" part. Everyone's clothes were patched, and sometimes there wasn't as much food on the table as he would like. There would have been more if his sons didn't throw so much at each another. But they all kept on growing, so his wife was probably right.

One day, Peter said to his wife, "Mr. Doyle has a cow I think we should buy."

Mr. Doyle sold livestock.

"Can we afford a cow, Peter?" asked his wife.

"It will eat the grass that grows in the meadow, and give us milk," said Peter.

"Yes, but do we have enough money?"

"I can pay half now, and the other half when the harvest comes."

"Peter, you will worry every day about paying Mr. Doyle, and it will make you unhappy."

Mr. Doyle had a reputation for being a hard man. Not many people were glad to see him when he came knocking at their door.

"I'll try not to worry. We'd be better off if we had a cow. Maybe we could even sell some of the milk. If only we had more money, I wouldn't have to worry about everything. Maybe this cow will help."

The cow was a good one. It ate the grass that grew in the meadow, and gave them plenty of milk. But when the harvest came, and Peter took his grain to market, he didn't get as much money as he had hoped. He didn't have enough to pay Mr. Doyle.

The day after Peter sold his grain, he saw through the window a heavy set man walking up the path that led to the farmhouse door. The door shook with three loud knocks from the head of a walking cane, and Peter opened it.

"Good morning, Peter. I trust you've been expecting my visit, and are prepared to pay me the money you owe."

It was Mr. Doyle.

"I can only pay part of it," said Peter. "It's all the money I have, except for what I saved to buy seed for next year's crops. But I will get the rest for you, I promise. If only you'll give me more time."

"More time? The money is due today. If you don't pay, you'll have to give me back my cow."

Peter clenched his jaw. Then he took a deep breath, and said in a quiet voice, "I will get the cow."

Peter went outside, leaving Mr. Doyle alone in the kitchen. The large man looked around. There were six chairs and a table made from unfinished wood. Some of the chairs had broken seats that had been repaired with ropes. The only other things in the room were a fireplace and a large iron pot.

As Mr. Doyle looked around the room, Rose stuck her head through the door. She kept her body behind the wall so all Mr. Doyle could see was her face. She stared at him until he began to frown. Her eyes laughed. She had eyes just like her mother's.

"When you frown, you look like a frog," she said.

A muscle on the left side Mr. Doyle's face twitched. He watched her smile get bigger and bigger, and the twitching in his cheek grew worse.

Suddenly, Rose burst out, "A frog! A frog! A frog!" She jumped out from behind the door, and danced around Mr. Doyle's legs.

"Stop that! Are you making fun of me?"

"Yes."

"You're just a little girl. What right do you have to make fun of me?"

"Because you're funny."

"Why?"

"Because you're pretending to be angry. I like you. Except now I don't, because you made the frog go away. I want to see the frog again."

Rose resumed her dance, shouting, "A frog! A frog!" in the hopes of bringing back the frog face.

"Stop!"

"I won't stop until you make the frog come back."

"There is no frog," said Mr. Doyle. "But if you stop your twirling, I will balance a spoon on my chin."

Rose stopped. That was worth seeing.

When Peter returned, Mr. Doyle was sitting on the floor with a doll in his lap, and Rose was singing to him with the serious expression children wear when they perform for an audience. When the song was over, Mr. Doyle clapped his hands, and Rose curtsied. He looked over at Peter, who was waiting by the door, and studied Peter's face.

"I've brought the cow," said Peter.

Mr. Doyle pursed his lips.

"When are you going to buy your seed for next year's planting?" he asked.

"Next month."

"Which market?"

"I always go to the Shrewsbury market."

"Go to Knightsbridge, and go first thing tomorrow morning. I know it's twice as far as Shrewsbury, but you'll be glad you went. I've been told the seed sellers have come early to Knightsbridge, and far more than the usual number. They're all trying to get rid of their seed at once, and you'll get it for half the usual price. With the money you save, you'll pay me what you owe."

"Will it be enough?" asked Peter.

"Go tomorrow, and let's see what you can do at Knightsbridge. Listen to me, Peter, I hate being so hard, but if I weren't, I'd never get paid. Go to Knightsbridge, then come and see me. We'll get everything straightened out. And if you want to do something extra, here's what I'd like. Let your little girl come visit with my Emily. She's just her age. Goodbye, Peter. Goodbye, Sweetheart.

It was a long journey to the Knightsbridge market, but

Mr. Doyle had been right. Peter got lots of good seed for next year's planting, and there was plenty of money left over to pay for the cow. The next day, Peter and Mr. Doyle sat together watching Rose and Emily play, and Peter thought that Mr. Doyle was a different person than he had imagined.

"Rose saw it," thought Peter.

* * *

As Peter's sons grew older, they helped more on the farm, and together they coaxed the rocky piece of land to bring forth the grain with greater generosity. But even though Peter brought more grain to market, he didn't come home with more money. The fact is, Peter didn't know much about business, and his appearance in the market acted like a signal for all the dishonest dealers to come forth at once.

"Peter!" called one of the grain dealers when Peter came to sell his crop. "Come over here. Let's talk. You know that I'm an honest man."

Peter didn't know anything about it, but he thought it would be rude to disagree.

"And you know that all I want to do is help you," said the grain dealer.

Peter wasn't sure what to say, so he nodded his head.

"But you've grown barley again, haven't you?" said the grain dealer.

"Barley is what grows best on my land."

"People don't want barley this year, Peter. They want wheat. If you had some wheat, I'd have to give you anything you asked. I'm too kind for my own good, Peter, and I'm sure you'd take the shirt right off my back for your wheat."

"Oh, no. I'd never do that."

"Have you got any wheat?"

"No."

"Just barley?"

"Yes."

"I'll give you twenty silver pieces for it."

"Twenty silver pieces!"

"Only because I'm a fool. Not everybody would do the same. Barley's hard to get rid of this year, and you know the barley that grows on your land isn't the best. But I'm too generous for my own good, and I don't care. I'm going to give you twenty silver pieces for that barley, even if I lose money in the bargain. But you've got to take it now, because I might change my mind. Now that I think of it, I'm not sure the barley is worth more than fifteen."

Peter thought his barley was worth more than twenty silver pieces, but the grain dealer kept saying he was an honest man. Peter was afraid he might get even less from the others. Besides, he didn't want to offend this man, who said the offer was made in kindness.

So Peter sold his barley for twenty silver pieces, and wondered why he always seemed to get so little for all his hard work.

Usually when he felt bad, Peter went straight home to be comforted by his wife, but today he chose a longer route back. Overhead, dark clouds threatened rain, but Peter didn't care. He wanted time to think.

He wondered if his life would always be this way. He hated to worry all the time, but the world was a dangerous place. Ruin lurked everywhere. If only he were rich, he thought, then he could be happy.

Close to Peter's house, across the fields of a neighbor's farm, lay a great forest. Some people said it was haunted, but Peter didn't believe it. Still, the forest gave him a strange feeling whenever he passed it, and like everyone else, he kept his distance.

Today, however, he walked straight toward the dark line of trees that stood beneath the leaden sky. *I'll show them*, he thought, without quite knowing what he meant. He was tired of the marketplace. He was tired of his stony farm. He was tired of worrying about rain and sun and plow and seed.

He left the road, and cut across a newly harvested field of corn. The reapers had come with their scythes, and the cut stems stuck out of the ground like shafts of broken spears. Peter stepped between the sharp stalks. The workers had been careless, and Peter saw wasted corn scattered on the ground. He thought about his own farm, and the dangers of the coming winter. Preoccupied with visions of cold barns and leaky roofs, Peter reached the far side of the field, and entered the woods.

From the outside, the forest looked menacing, but inside, a harmony of dusky colors mingled with the toasted smell of fall. As evening settled in, the wind rustled the dry leaves on the ground. The sky was getting darker. Birds stopped calling to one another. All was quiet. The forest was waiting.

Peter didn't notice. His head was too full of catastrophes

that might or might not happen. Phantom dangers swarmed among his thoughts, distracting him, consuming him, and blinding him to the real danger that lay just ahead.

It's unwise for a man to ignore the living world around him, and make his home among the unquiet ghosts of his fears. Peter wandered off the forest path, and came to a part of the woods where few humans had ever traveled before. Without even realizing it, he came to a place where magic hung in the air, and he stepped right into the middle of a fairy ring.

Not many people know when they've stepped into a fairy ring. They're hard to see. Grown ups almost never see them, but children with sharp eyes can. Sometimes flowers grow around them, and the pattern hints at the hidden ring. They're more likely to be found in shady places than sunny ones, but not all the time. Usually, moss can be found nearby, because moss grows best in solemn places. But no two fairy rings are the same, so it's hard to say what one might look like. Those who can see them just know.

Peter didn't know. He stood unaware in the fairy ring, thinking about a shirt he had bought that had fallen apart the third time he wore it. He had hoped the shirt would last for years.

"It's easy for people to cheat me," he thought, "because I never know when someone is being dishonest."

What could he do? His mind wrestled with the problem.

"If only I knew what people were really like," he thought, "then it wouldn't be so easy for them."

That was it. Peter had found the key to the riddle.

"I wish I had a way of knowing what people were really like."

Peter had been staring at the ground with his lips pushed forward, and his brow all wrinkled as he thought his way through the problem. Now he looked up, and noticed something shiny at the foot of a nearby tree. He walked over to the tree, knelt down, and examined the object. It was a tiny spyglass.

A spyglass is like a telescope, but it's used for looking at things that are closer than stars. Sailors use them to look at ships in the distance, and generals use them to watch the enemy. Peter picked it up. It was no bigger than his finger, and looked like a toy. He wondered what it was doing here in the woods. It was brightly polished with no sign of rust, and as far as he could tell, it was just an ordinary spyglass. But Peter didn't know he had been standing in a fairy ring. He didn't know the spyglass was magic.

All spyglasses have some magic in them. How else can they make things that are far away appear close? If you ask scientists how they work, they might say words like "refraction," and "magnification," and talk about the bending of light. But if they're honest scientists, they will admit that they don't really, *really* know how it happens. "Refraction" and "magnification" are useful words, and they help scientists do wonderful things, but they don't take away the magic from a glass that holds the secret of how to bend the airy beams of light.

The spyglass that Peter held in his hand contained even more magic than most spyglasses—quite a bit more. This spyglass was enchanted. The wish Peter had made while standing in the fairy ring had been granted. Wishing inside a fairy ring doesn't always make the wish come true, but something peculiar is bound to happen. It's a dangerous thing to do, and should be avoided whenever possible. Treasures found in the land of Faerie are not always what they seem.

Peter put the spyglass in his pocket, found his way back to the forest path, and from there to the main road. As he walked, he saw a man coming in the opposite direction. The man was too far away for Peter to tell who he was, and Peter thought this would be a good opportunity to try out the spyglass. He took it out, and this time he noticed there was an inscription engraved on one side. It said,

> the eyes deceive it love is gone
> to see things right then use me wrong

The inscription looked like it was written in a foreign language. Peter puzzled over it, but couldn't make out its meaning. He shrugged, and put the spyglass up to his eye.

The glass made the man on the road look close, and Peter saw a face with a heavy forehead and hungry eyes. The man's lips were thin, and he licked them with the tip of his tongue. He was unshaven with short bristles that grew in patches over his face, making Peter think of a wild beast. All of a sudden, Peter recognized him. It was Jarvis; but Jarvis as he had never seen him before.

After a few minutes of walking, the two men met.

"Hello, Peter," said Jarvis. "I'm glad to see you. I've been thinking of doing someone a good turn today, and I can't think of anyone better than you."

Now that they were close, Peter removed the spyglass from his eye, and saw the old familiar face he was used to. Jarvis was the same friendly-looking fellow he had always been. Peter put the spyglass up to his eye again.

This time the spyglass didn't make Jarvis look closer, but once again it distorted his face, making Peter jump with surprise.

"What's the matter, Peter? You look like you've seen a ghost. What's that in your hand?"

"Just something I found in the woods."

"It looks like a toy. That's lucky for your little daughter, isn't it? She'll have fun with it. Well, here's something that's lucky for you. I know a man who needs to get rid of a horse. It's a fine horse. You know I wouldn't say it, if it wasn't true. She looks a little run down, but that's a good thing, because it means you can get her cheap. If word gets out just how cheap this horse is, she'll be snapped up in a second, so there's not much time. I know it's late, but what do you say we go and see if we can be the first ones to make an offer? Trust me, this is the best deal you're going to see all year, and you'd be a fool to miss it."

All the while Jarvis spoke, Peter had been thinking about the face he had seen through the spyglass. He realized that Jarvis was lying about the horse. It wasn't a good horse at all.

"No," said Peter. And he walked away.

Peter didn't tell anyone about the spyglass, but he kept it with him all the time. Before he bought or sold anything, he used the spyglass to examine the man he did business with. He learned how to hide it in his hand, so that people couldn't tell what he was doing. As he brought it up to his eye, he pretended to scratch his forehead. The spyglass told him everything that was bad about a person, and it wasn't long before Peter became the sharpest trader in the whole market.

Peter was getting more for the crops that grew on his farm, and paying less for the things he bought. That meant he had extra money, and he thought less about putting food on the table, and more about getting things he wanted. Every week he thought of something new, and today he was searching the market for a horse. He had been talking to all the horse dealers, but none of them had an animal that would suit him. He was just getting ready to go home for the day, when he heard a familiar voice at his shoulder.

"Peter! Where have you been? If I didn't know better, I'd think you were avoiding me."

It was Jarvis.

"It's too bad you missed out on that horse I told you about last time we met. But you seem to have nothing but good luck, because today I've got a horse for you that's better than anything you've ever seen."

"No thanks, Jarvis."

"Just come and look at him. He's the finest animal you'll ever meet, and it will make you happy just to gaze on the beast."

Peter thought it couldn't hurt to look. They walked a short distance to where the horse was tied up, and indeed, it was worth seeing. The horse had a reddish brown body with a black mane and a black tail. It had a long, curved neck, and a strong back. The horse stood as still as a statue. Its eyes were calm and sleepy, in contrast to the powerful lines of its body. Peter stroked the horse's neck. It was a beautiful animal.

"How much do you want for him?" asked Peter.

Jarvis named a price that Peter could just afford. The horse pushed its velvet nose into Peter's hand.

"This looks like a very good horse," thought Peter. "Maybe Jarvis has changed. Maybe I can trust him now."

Peter reached into his pocket for the money, and his fingers touched the spyglass. He took it out, pretended to scratch his forehead, and looked.

He saw the heavy brow, the darting eyes, and the thin, dry lips. Peter drew in his breath as he looked at the cunning expression. He took the glass away from his eye, and looked again at the beautiful horse. He wasn't sure what to do.

"Wait one moment, Jarvis. I'll be right back."

Peter knew someone who could help him.

A few minutes later Peter returned, accompanied by his friend, John Forge. John had fought in the king's cavalry many years ago, and he knew something about horses. He had gray hair, and moved more slowly than he used to in the days when he rode with the army, but his shoulders were still broad, and he held himself as straight as a bayonet.

He narrowed his keen eyes, as he looked at Jarvis. John didn't think much of Jarvis, and was suspicious of any horse Jarvis would try to sell. John examined the horse's mouth, teeth, coat, and hooves, but could find nothing wrong with it. He untied the horse, and walked a short distance with it. There was a tiny stumble as one of the horse's hooves brushed against the ground. That might not mean anything; maybe the horse was stiff from standing in one place for too long, but it could be important. John looked closely at the horse's eyes. He saw a slight droop of the eyelids, and the eyes themselves were glassy. John glared at Jarvis.

"This animal's been drugged," he said. "He probably rears or bites when his head is clear. What kind of game are you playing, Jarvis? I'll wager you're trying to sell a half-wild horse."

John walked over to Peter.

"If I'm right, Peter, this horse is worth barely half of what Jarvis is asking. It would take months of training to get him into any kind of shape for you to ride."

John gave Jarvis a hard look, and walked away.

"You tried to cheat me!" said Peter.

Jarvis squirmed. "Shhhh! Keep your voice down, you idiot!"

"You tried to sell me a wild horse!"

"Quiet, I tell you! If anyone hears, I'm ruined!"

"You're a cheat!"

"It was an honest mistake, Peter. You know me, I'd never try to cheat you."

"Yes I do know you, and you tried to sell me a wild, drugged horse! You're a crook!"

"Peter, Peter. That's enough. Here, take the horse. Give me whatever you want for it. Just be quiet."

Peter was angry that Jarvis believed he was fool enough to buy a half-wild horse. He reached into his pocket, and felt a few small coins. He threw them on the ground at Jarvis's feet.

"There! There is your price for the horse, you cheat!"

Jarvis looked in dismay at the coins on the ground.

"But Peter, that's nothing at all."

"I don't care! I'll tell the whole town what you tried to do."

"No, Peter, no. We've always been friends. Let's think of the horse as my gift to you. You know I've always been a generous man. Too generous for my own good, maybe, but I can't help it."

Peter wasn't listening. He was walking away with his new horse.

When the drugs wore off, the horse was indeed wild, and Peter had to hire a man to come train it. It took a long time, and cost Peter some money, but in the end he had a fine horse. Even when he counted the money he had spent for the training, Peter had gotten a bargain. He rode the best horse in town, and it hadn't cost him much more than an ordinary one.

Peter walked alone one evening, rolling the tiny spyglass between his finger and thumb. He thought about Jarvis and the horse, and his conscience pricked him. He wondered if he had taken advantage of Jarvis. Jarvis had been so frightened that he had been willing to sell the horse for almost nothing.

Peter had never known what it was like to have an uneasy conscience. He had gone through life feeling that others were taking advantage of him, and wishing he could do something about it. Now, with the help of the spyglass, Peter had turned the tables, and he wasn't sure he liked the way it felt.

"Jarvis has cheated me again and again. All I did was get back a little of my own. That's all. Only a little of what's owed to me."

He thought of the fine horse. He couldn't bear the thought of giving it up.

"People like Jarvis deserve to know what it feels like to have someone else get the better of them. Maybe now he won't be so quick to cheat others. I did him a favor."

Deep inside, Peter knew it wasn't true, but he was determined to keep the horse, so he fought against the feeling. He fought so hard that he defeated that feeling completely. He looked down at the spyglass, which he continued to roll between his finger and thumb.

"I'll show them," he said.

* * *

At first, Peter had used the spyglass to find those who were honest, but now he used it to find people who were dishonest. He looked through the glass at every man he met, and the uglier he appeared, the better Peter was pleased. He found out their villainies, and he used the knowledge to get anything he wanted from them.

Peter lost interest in farming. He left that sort of work to his sons. He even lost interest in the animals who lived behind the farmhouse. One by one they all ran away. Peter traveled to the great trading centers of the land, and sought out the worst men in every place he went. He battled with them to get the upper hand, but it was an unfair battle, because he had the spyglass. He became more and more skilled in it's use, and he learned how to discover all that a man tried to hide. Peter became rich.

Being rich was what Peter had always dreamed of, and he tried to convince himself he was happy. He no longer worried about having enough food for his family, or whether the roof of the barn would collapse, but a hundred new worries had replaced each of the old ones. Peter spent so much time with dishonest men, that he came to believe that no one could be trusted. No one in the world could sniff out evil like Peter, but he had lost his ability to see good. He suspected everyone, and his mind could find no rest.

Peter had become like a creature of the night, whose round eyes pierce the murky darkness, but are blinded by the light of day. Peter saw every slightest shade of dishonesty, but his eyes slipped over the good that was all around him without even noticing it was there.

"At least I'm happy at home," he said to himself.

But even Peter's home had changed. He thought his

family looked at him differently. There was something in their faces that Peter had never seen before. He tried to believe it was only his imagination, but he couldn't, and the strange expressions he saw froze his heart.

The truth was that Peter's family loved him as much as ever, but they could tell he was unhappy. They saw he was sick inside, and they saw that the disease was getting worse. But they didn't know what to do.

One night Peter sat by the window with the spyglass in his hand. Outside, pouring rain darkened the sky. Peter could see nothing except a curtain of water, shaken now and then by powerful gusts of wind. The walls of the room were stained red by the glow of a dying fire.

Peter looked down at the spyglass. It reflected the gray world outside the window with a cold, metallic shine.

"I would be nothing without you," thought Peter. "I would be defenseless, and no man would hesitate to crush me."

And yet, the desolate world the spyglass revealed made him fear the tiny cylinder that lay in his hand.

When he first got it, he had used the spyglass only when he went to the market. He had the feeling that it didn't tell the whole truth about a person, so he never looked at his friends with it. But the more time he spent among dishonest men the more suspicious he became of everyone around him, and after some small disagreement with John Forge, he had turned the glass on him. After that, their friendship had withered away. But he had never used the spyglass on his family.

"I know who they are," he thought. "They're the ones who have always loved me. They're not perfect, because no one is. The spyglass shows only what is bad, so I won't look at them with it."

But a wall had grown up between Peter and his family. He thought about how much he had done for them. He had sacrificed everything: his rest, his happiness, and worst of all, his conscience. What more did they want?

The rain dashed against the window with a sound of beating drums.

Peter felt he had been cheated. He had done everything he could to make his family happy, and now there was that strange look in their eyes.

"They act as if they don't know me," he thought. "Maybe I have changed. I'm with villains every day, and if I don't stay sharp, they'll cheat me. That's the way of the world: beat or be beaten. But if I have changed, maybe they have, too. Why should they be any different from the rest? I don't expect them to be different. I'm a reasonable man. But I have a right to know who it is I live with."

Peter's eldest son came into the room, then hesitated. He saw Peter sitting in the shadows, and he could tell his father was troubled. The young man took a step forward, but there was something in his father's eyes that kept him back. Peter saw the hesitation, and the corners of his mouth turned down. Both were silent, then Peter's hand moved. It rose up until it reached its familiar position in front of his face. Peter pretended to scratch his forehead, and looked through the spyglass.

The next moment he dashed it to the ground, and ran from the house. Rain pelted him in the face, but Peter ran without direction or thought. He ran across wet fields, through ditches filled with water, and finally into the depths of the forest. Faster and faster he ran until something dark rose up in his path, and his head crashed against a heavy limb jutting out from an old tree. The collision shook the tree to its roots. Peter fell to the ground, and knew no more.

When Peter awoke, sunlight was streaming through his bedroom window. The sky had been washed clean by wind and rain, and the only remaining signs of the storm were a few wisps of gray clouds in the clearing sky. The trees reflected the yellow light of the rising sun. All the edges of the world were sharp, as if they had been scraped clean by the storm.

Peter's memory of the night before was uncertain. He remembered rain and darkness and sudden pain, but nothing else. He didn't know how he got home. On a table next to his bed sat a loaf of freshly baked bread, a dish of butter, and a bowl of strawberry jam. Peter cut a thick slice, and spread butter and jam on it.

"I wonder what happened to me," he thought as he chewed. "I wish I had died."

But he didn't really. The butter and jam tasted too good. He stretched his arms over his head, and thought about getting up, but the bed was soft, and the blankets were warm, so he leaned back against the pillows, and closed his eyes.

Then he remembered the spyglass. Where was it? He

remembered throwing it away from him last night. He had to find it, and make sure it was safe. It was the most valuable thing he owned. But just as he was about to get out of bed, he stopped. He realized he didn't want the spyglass. The spyglass showed only a half truth, and a half truth is worse than a lie, because the part that's true makes the lie easier to believe. The spyglass was powerful, but it was bad.

"I'd better find it, and take it back to the woods," he thought.

He got out of bed, and walked into the kitchen. His daughter was there, and he held her in his arms for the first time in months. She had something in her hands she was playing with. It was small and shiny.

"Look what I found, Daddy," she said. "I wonder what it is."

It was the spyglass. She tilted her head, and squinted her eyes, as her lips mouthed the words,

"The eyes deceive if love is gone. To see things right, then use me wrong."

She held it up to her eye.

"No!" screamed Peter. "Put it down! Throw it away!"

But it was too late. Rose looked through the spyglass, gazing around the room. She gasped.

"How beautiful," she whispered.

She ran to the window.

"Come and look! I think it must be magic!"

She held the spyglass to Peter, and he noticed something odd. She had been looking through the wrong end. If you look through the wrong end of an ordinary spyglass, it doesn't make things appear closer, it makes them appear farther away. Peter put the spyglass to his eye the way his daughter had, and looked.

The world was transformed. Peter saw the freshness of the earth multiplied a thousand times over, until the beauty penetrated into his soul, and he felt as if his heart would break. He looked around the room he had known for so many years. He wanted to hug the pots and pans that hung above the fire. They were the most jolly, friendly pots and pans he had ever seen. All the things he saw showed him their secret truths.

When he had looked at everything, and understood everything, the last thing he did was to point the spyglass at his daughter. He laughed. He saw exactly what he knew he would. She looked just the same as always.

THE PRINCESS AND THE GOATHERD

There once was a king and a queen who were as handsome and beautiful as all kings and queens should be. They attended balls, vacationed in far away places, and kept up with all the latest fashions. The king's vests were embroidered with gold, and the queen wore fur coats made from the rarest creatures in the world. As the Royal Exchequer said on numerous occasions, it was a good thing the treasury was full.

One day the queen told the king that she would like to have a child.

"Everyone's doing it these days," she said.

"I thought everyone was training parrots," said the king.

"That was last month," said the queen.

"Then by all means, let us have a child," said the king.

Not long after, a princess was born, and was given the name Claire. She had little, pink fingers and tiny, pink toes.

The queen was charmed.

But in addition to her little fingers and tiny toes, the princess also had a good pair of lungs, and as soon as she discovered what they were for, she filled them with air, and let out a howl.

The queen was not charmed at all.

They put the princess in a cradle of the most fashionable design, but she still continued to cry at the most inconvenient times of day and night. After putting up with the noise for more than a week, the king and queen decided it was time for something to be done.

"How can we live with a creature that shrieks every time she wants something?" asked the queen. "She's impossible. Everything must be done her way, or she screams unceasingly."

"I couldn't agree with you more," said the king. "It's unendurable. If you want my opinion, I say we send her back."

"I don't think we can do that," said the queen.

"Well then, let's drown her."

"In this weather? We'd surely catch cold."

"Have one of the servants do it," said the king.

"I've already asked. They all refused."

"Then I suppose we'll have to live with her. But at least let's put her down in the coal cellar. That way the crying won't be so loud."

As the king predicted, the sound of Claire's crying was muffled by the stone walls of the coal cellar, but it wasn't a perfect solution. Whenever people came to congratulate the king and queen on the birth of their new child, they had to be taken down to the cellar in order to actually have a look at her. After a while, it became embarrassing.

"I don't like the way they raise their eyebrows," said the queen. "I find it offensive."

"So do I," said the king. "I'm afraid we'll have to bring her out. We can't have people talking, you know."

"But the noise! Whatever will we do?"

"Let us travel south, and take up our residence by the sea. We'll lie on the beach, swim in the waves, and come back when she stops crying."

"How long will that be?"

"Two years. Longer if the weather is nice."

"But I'll need an entirely new wardrobe," said the queen.

"So shall I," said the king.

The weather by the sea was delightful, and there were so many parties and balls that seven years went by before the king and queen remembered they had a daughter who had never been properly introduced to her parents.

"I suppose we had better go back," said the queen.

"But it's the beginning of the horse races," complained the king. "Why am I always the one who has to sacrifice?"

"Because you are the king."

"I fail to see the logic."

"Well, I won't argue the point. We shall stay for the races, and after that the Grand Ball, and after that we'll see," said the queen.

* * *

Although the king and queen had left the palace before their daughter was even one month old, they had given instructions that she should be treated well. In fact, they had told the palace servants that in order to make sure she didn't miss her parents too much, she should be given everything she wanted. As time went on, Princess Claire wanted a great many things.

"Why are all my toys so old?" she asked one day.

"They are not old at all," said her nursemaid. "Why, just this week you have had three new dolls and a stuffed rabbit."

"I'm tired of them. Take them away, and burn them. Why don't I have any friends?"

"Your cousin will come visit you next month. You know what an agreeable playmate she is."

"I don't like my cousin. Why don't I have any parents? My cousin has parents, and she says they love her."

"You do have parents, dearest. It's just that they're away at the moment."

"Send for them immediately."

So the king and queen were sent for. They both heaved a sigh, and admitted it was time to end their holiday, and return home.

"Why have you been away for so long, and why are you so fat?" asked the princess when she saw her father for the first time.

"How little you have changed," said the king.

Claire turned to the queen, and studied her with narrowed eyes.

"It's a shame you're so old," she said at last.

"Let us return to the seashore," said the queen.

But by this time the royal treasury was not as full as it used to be, so they had to content themselves with attending parties every night, and spending as little time as possible with their daughter.

*   *   *

When Princess Claire said she had no friends, she was telling the literal truth. She spent most of her days by herself in the palace nursery, or playing in the gardens. One day, she was running after a peacock, trying to scare it into opening its feathers, when she heard a sniffling noise, like the sound of someone crying. It was coming from behind a fountain. The princess went to investigate, and found a young goatherd hiding in the bushes.

"What are you doing here?" she said. "Leave immediately. This park belongs to me, and I won't have it soiled by the likes of you."

"I don't know where to go," said the boy.

"Go home, of course."

"I'm afraid to go home."

"Afraid to go home? You must be the biggest coward in the world. I have never been afraid to go home, and I can't imagine that it ever took much bravery on my part. Once I was afraid to go sailing in the royal yacht, but that was during a terrible storm. And it *was* a storm no matter what my lying cousin says."

"But if I go home, I'll be beaten," said the goatherd. "I fell asleep in the meadow, and all my goats have run away."

"Then buy some more. Are you as dull-witted as you are cowardly?"

"I have no money."

Now it happened that the princess had a gold coin in her pocket that her father had given her to buy a new dress. There was to be a ball next week, and the princess planned to wear a dress that would outshine her cousin's. Unfortunately, the royal treasury was not at all what it used to be, and gold coins from her father were hard to come by.

She looked at the goatherd. He was about her own age, and she could see how frightened he was. Her hand moved toward her pocket. Then she imagined the upcoming ball and the old dress everyone had seen her wear just last month. The princess hesitated.

Off in the distance she saw her father taking his daily walk through a grove of pear trees. His hair had been dressed by the royal hairdresser that morning, and each strand lay perfectly in its place. His brightly colored clothes were fresh from the tailor, and had been made of the finest silks.

The princess reached into her pocket, and took out the gold coin. It flashed in the sun, and the eyes of the goatherd were dazzled by the light. When he realized what it was, his mouth fell open.

The princess put the coin into the boy's hand, and smiled to see his jaw hanging down in such a silly way. The goatherd looked into the eyes of the girl who had saved him, and strange to say, he saw something there that made his mouth open even wider. The princess laughed, turned on her heel, and ran back to the palace.

* * *

"Father, this is the least disappointing party I have ever had. I know that you're filling the bottles of champagne with the miserable stuff from our vineyards, and you pretend the cheese from the dairy is imported, but still, it's not nearly as bad as the parties you usually give me."

"I'm glad you're pleased, my dear. Your mother and I have waited for this day to come for many years. You are seventeen years old today, and soon you will be married, and off our hands forever."

This piece of information came as a surprise to the princess. But she didn't think she'd mind moving out of the palace, so she said,

"Well, if it must be, find me a husband who is more handsome than the one my cousin has."

The king didn't think it would be easy to find his daughter a husband of any description, let alone a handsome one, so he consulted the Royal Academy of Distinguished Scholars to see if they had any suggestions. The scholars put their heads together, and argued for two whole days. When they finally stopped debating, the Chief

Scholar stepped forward to announce their conclusions.

"We approach the problem from a systems point of view, Your Majesty," the Chief Scholar said. "The princess does not exist in isolation, and it is necessary to understand the various pathways that lead to the desired state of matrimony. Basing our hypothesis on this model, and allowing ourselves to be influenced by suggestive results from experiments performed by those in similar circumstances, we recommend a large dowry."

"A large dowry! Will the treasury bear it?"

"That is a question of *fact*, not of *theory*. As such, it is outside our realm of expertise."

The Royal Exchequer was consulted, who stated that the answer to the question of *fact* was no, the treasury would not bear it. So the king passed a law requiring all the nobles to contribute half their land to the princess's dowry, and word was sent abroad that a rich princess might be willing to consider a proposal of marriage, if a suitable candidate thought it worthwhile to ask.

Kings and princes in need of money poured into the palace to meet Princess Claire. None of them stayed for more than half an hour.

"Can't you make yourself agreeable for even a single day?" asked the king.

"Why should I? They're only interested in the money. They don't care a straw about me."

"Nobody cares a straw about you."

"Nevertheless, I think my husband should."

The king was wrong when he said that nobody cared

about the princess. The goatherd whom the princess had saved many years ago never forgot her kindness. He thought about her often, and sometimes at night he caught glimpses of her in his dreams. When he heard that none of the kings or princes would marry her, and that they had all gone home, he decided he would try his own luck.

He presented himself at the palace, and asked to speak with the princess. The palace guards didn't know what to do. It was highly irregular for a goatherd to seek the hand of a princess, but the kings and princes were all gone, and it seemed unlikely that anyone else would come. They decided to take him to the king to see what he thought about it.

The king was enraged at the idea of a goatherd proposing to become his son-in-law.

"At least let me see her," said the goatherd to the king, "so that I may ask her if she loves me. I know it's unlikely because she's a princess and I'm only a goatherd, but love cares nothing for rank."

"Humph!" said the king. "The princess has lived her entire life without love, and at this point I believe it would be a mistake to expose her to it. It's like people who are unaccustomed to eating coconuts. It's unwise for them to develop the habit later in life. It's are almost certain to disagree with them."

The king was so offended by the idea of the goatherd falling in love with his daughter that he told the guards to throw him into the deepest dungeon, and keep him there for the rest of his life. The palace guards seized the young man, and marched him away.

They made him walk down narrow, winding staircases lit by smoky torches. Deeper and deeper they went. When there were no more staircases, he had to climb down a long, shaky ladder, then another, and then another. At last they reached the lowest dungeon, deep within the earth. They pushed the goatherd into a small cell, and slammed the door behind him with a clang.

The goatherd looked around. The walls of the dungeon were made of stone, and skeletons of former prisoners lay scattered across the floor. There were no tables or chairs, or even a bed, only a pile of rags in one corner for him to sleep on.

He sat down on the stone floor, and thought how much nicer it would be to sit on a soft couch next to the princess, but that didn't seem likely. He wondered how the king would like being shut up in a prison, and wished with all his heart they could trade places, so the king could find out for himself. For more than a month he sat on the floor, wishing he could be with the princess, and dreaming of the terrible things he'd like to do to the king.

In the middle of the dungeon was a drain that was covered with a metal grate. One day, green slime began to ooze from the drain. It smelled like rotting Brussels sprouts, and the goatherd wished more than ever that he was out of that awful place.

The slime oozed from the drain all day long. It spread over the floor, and by nightfall it had reached the walls of the goatherd's cell. Still it came, filling the room, until the goatherd said to himself,

"If I don't do something, I'll drown in this awful muck."

The bones of the former prisoners that had been lying on the floor were now floating on the surface of the slime. The goatherd picked up two of them, waded over to the door, and banged on it.

"Maybe someone will hear, and come help me," he thought. "At the very least I might disturb the sleep of the cruel jailer who feeds me nothing but bread and water."

So he banged on the door, and soon a rhythm arose. The goatherd liked the way it sounded, so he banged harder and faster. He banged on the door, he banged on the walls, and he banged on the skulls that floated on the rising slime. The dungeon filled with the rhythms of the goatherd's drumming. The walls shook, and the green slime vibrated in time to the beat.

Far above the dungeon the princess lay in her bed. She woke from her sleep, and heard the pounding of the goatherd's music. She couldn't tell where it came from, and thought it was the sound of her own heart beating.

"I didn't know I had a heart," she said to herself.

There was a feeling of emptiness inside her that made her chest ache.

"I don't know if I like having a heart," she thought.

The green ooze bubbled and splashed as the goatherd beat faster and faster. It flew into the air like a fountain, and the goatherd saw it form itself into fantastic shapes. He saw trees with branches made of flying goo. There were animals and birds, and then right above the drain the ooze bubbled furiously. Something emerged from the slime, and the goatherd saw a red ball on top of a green stem. It was a rosebud. The goatherd stopped drumming, the green liquid became still, and the rose opened its petals.

The smell of the green slime faded away, and was replaced by the smell of warm earth, baking in the summer sun, and the flowery scent of the rose. The goatherd looked at the flower in amazement, reached out his hand, and plucked it.

There was a gurgling sound, and everything began to spin. The goatherd flew around and around the prison. Faster and faster he went in ever smaller circles, until at last he was sucked right down the drain. He felt himself moving at a terrible speed; first one way then another, as he flew through pipe after pipe, and then all of a sudden he plopped down onto the ground right in front of his own cottage. The rose was gone. In the goatherd's hand was a compass made of two glass domes held together by a ring of red gold. The goatherd stood up, put the compass in his pocket, wiped off as much of the slime as he could, and went to see how his goats were getting along.

* * *

"I'm surprised you're still here," said the king to his daughter, as he sat down to his breakfast of poached eggs and bacon. "I really would have thought you'd be married by now."

"Evidently not," said the princess.

"I knew it wouldn't be easy, but I thought the

extravagant generosity I showed with regard to your dowry would have done the trick."

The king pushed a piece of bacon into his mouth.

"It's a burden to have a child like you," he said through the mouthful of crispy meat. "Now I will have to eat nothing but caviar for a week in order to restore my spirits."

The princess glared at him.

"I hope it will make you a better father," she said. "At any rate, if you intend to get rid of me, I have decided that I should like a husband who loves me. You know that I have never been aquatinted with love, and I don't know whether I have missed it. But I've heard that people like it, and I intend to give it a try. When you find a husband for me, Father, please make sure he loves me."

"Highly unlikely, and a bad idea, anyway. When people are in love, you never know what they'll do. They act in unpredictable ways, and it's all terribly irregular. I've seen people in love who ignore all the world entirely, and completely forget their manners. Love is best left to the peasants, who have no manners anyway."

The king wiped the egg off his beard, and went to consult with his Royal Distinguished Scholars.

The scholars all looked grave. The difficulties involved in getting the princess married were worse than they had thought. They decided to organize a colloquium, and took over the best wing of the palace so they could debate undisturbed. They told the king they would need a large dinner every night, and plenty of wine. After a week they declared themselves ready to reveal the results of their deliberations.

"We are only beginning to understand the core elements that propel the progression of events that would lead to a proposal of matrimony for the princess," the Chief Scholar explained. "Such core elements include admiration, affection, and esteem. If we accept that these are determining long-term factors, it gives us a diversity of novel approaches that might impact on the underlying processes. I think we have every reason to be hopeful."

"Get to the point," growled the king. The scholars had drunk up a great deal of his wine, and he was in a bad mood.

"We suggest hiring artists to paint pictures that celebrate her beauty, and poets to write verses extolling her soul. Such things may kindle the flames of passion."

Word was sent forth, gold was offered, and poets and painters came in crowds. Unfortunately, they were unable to capture the finer elements of the princess. The painters began by flattering her, which made her sneer. The poets were all so thin and soulful-looking that the princess found it hard to resist the temptation to bump into them, and watch them fly across the room. So the painters and poets, being true to their art, produced portraits and poems that were of little use.

"Now what?" asked the king.

"Since the true artists have failed, perhaps those of a more, shall we say, amateur breed, will serve us better," said the Chief Scholar.

"What if they don't want to?"

"Force them."

So the king passed a law requiring each of his subjects to paint a picture of the princess, and write a poem about her, too. The people grumbled a great deal, but a law is a law, so they did what they could with paint and pen. They should have saved themselves the trouble. The paintings were awful, and when the poems were read aloud, the palace dogs howled.

There was one painting, however, that was different from the rest. It showed the princess as beautiful as a goddess. She took one look at it, and declared that it was rubbish. She said that it didn't look like her at all, but still, she thought she might like to meet the man who had painted it.

"Impossible," said the king. "It's that pest of a goatherd who says he's in love with you. How he got out of the royal dungeon I'll never know. But you needn't worry, because I ordered the guards to take him to the center of the Thousand Mile Desert, and leave him there to die."

The king heaved a sigh.

"There's a lesson here for all of us," he said. "Though I can't imagine what it might be."

The goatherd had also written a poem which the princess snatched away before anyone could see it. She carried it out to the palace gardens, and sat down near a fountain to read. The fountain must have splashed it, because when she got back, some of the ink was smeared.

The beautiful painting was sent around to the kings and princes. The poem didn't accompany it because the princess said she lost it. When the kings and princes saw the painting, many of them decided to come back for another look. None of them stayed more than fifteen minutes.

Meanwhile, the king's soldiers had tied up the goatherd, flung him across the back of a camel, and carried him to the center of the Thousand Mile Desert. When they arrived, they tossed him to the ground, and galloped away.

The goatherd struggled with the ropes. After a while he got them loose, and was able to free himself. He looked around, and saw the sea of sand stretch to the horizon in every direction. He saw neither tree nor bush. The goatherd didn't know what to do, so he sat down, crossed his legs, and rested his chin in the palms of his hands.

The wind began to blow, and sand swirled around the goatherd, but he didn't move.

"What's the point?" he said to himself. "It's very unlikely I'll ever marry the princess, so I might as well sit here and die."

The wind blew stronger, and sand got into his eyes and ears.

"Blow all you want," said the goatherd. "I said I'm not moving."

The wind blew harder and harder. The swirling sand formed itself into strange shapes. Sandy beasts roared from the storm. Lions, hyenas, and eagles, all made out of sand, formed themselves, disappeared, and formed themselves again, always threatening the goatherd with their talons and claws.

"Oh, this is really too much!" said the goatherd, and he

got up, and began to walk.

Blowing sand was everywhere, making it impossible for the goatherd to see more than a few feet in front of him. He couldn't tell where he was going, and he thought that for all he knew he might be walking in circles.

Then he remembered the compass. He took it out of his pocket, and examined it. The dial was completely blank. There were no markings to show which way was north or which way was south. But the needle pointed in some direction, so the goatherd made up his mind to follow it.

He walked and walked through the blowing sand, always following the direction of the compass. The sand was deep, and he slipped and stumbled as he made his way across the desert. At last, the wind stopped. All the sand had blown away, and the goatherd stood on firm rock.

It was night. The moon lit the landscape so that the goatherd could see everything around him as clearly as if it were day. Nearby, a cat walked over the rock on silent paws. It had green eyes and black fur. Attached to a collar around its neck was a leather pouch. The goatherd crouched down, and the cat walked over to him, and rested its paws on the goatherd's knee.

"What is it?" whispered the goatherd.

"Moon dust," said the cat. "Take it from my collar, and when you return home, sprinkle some on your doorstep as you would sprinkle seeds on the earth. That which grows will be invisible to all but you."

"How will I get home?" asked the goatherd, untying the pouch from the cat's neck.

But before the words were out of his mouth, he was standing at his door.

The goatherd opened the pouch, and sprinkled some of the moon dust on his doorstep. The dust was silvery, and it sparkled as it floated through the air. As soon as it touched the ground, the earth began to shake, and the goatherd jumped backward. Great towers rumbled upward. They pushed through the earth, and rose into the sky, sending dirt flying everywhere. In no time at all a castle stood where the goatherd's cottage used to be. The walls of the castle glowed with a pale light. Spires rose into the sky, reaching impossible heights, and at the top of the tallest spire of all was a small disk of gold.

The castle was furnished with thick carpets and soft chairs. Broad staircases led to balconies that overlooked echoing, marble vestibules, and ballrooms the size of small villages. One of the rooms was filled with leather books sitting on shelves that rose all the way up to the ceiling, ten stories above the goatherd's head. Next door to it was a crystal-domed conservatory where the was air was humid, and plants with broad leaves crowded together like trees in a jungle.

One of the hallways contained a little door, no more than three feet high. The goatherd crawled into it, and squeezed through a tunnel leading to a room that was so full of light that his eyes were nearly blinded. All around the room piles of diamonds, emeralds, and rubies lay in heaps as high as the goatherd's old cottage.

The banquet hall had tables hundreds of feet long that

were covered with dishes holding soups, meats, salads, and cakes. The goatherd sat down, and poured some wine into a goblet that had been cut from a diamond the size of his fist. He raised it to his lips, took a sip, then pushed it away.

"What do I care for food and drink, if I cannot marry the princess." he said to himself. He went upstairs, entered one of the bedrooms, and fell asleep on a mattress stuffed with the wool of moonlit clouds.

* * *

"Father," said the princess the next morning as she and the king rode in the royal carriage, "what is that castle there in the distance? It's more beautiful than anything I have ever seen. The towers sparkle boldly in the sun, and seem to touch the sky itself. Surely, it wasn't there yesterday. I wonder how such a thing came to be so suddenly."

"Your eyes place tricks on you," answered the king. "There's nothing but a bank of mist. I hope you're not developing an imagination. It's unbecoming, and you know how awful you are already."

The king sighed.

"Having children is a heavy burden. Now I will have to buy myself a new carriage in order to restore my spirits."

The goatherd slept well during the night, and in the morning he was full of hope. So once again he made his way to the palace, and asked to see the princess.

"You again!" said the king. "You are the most impertinent creature alive. Do you know what it cost to have you dragged to the Thousand Mile Desert? Why with the money I spent on camels alone I could have bought myself a new vest. It seems as if my life is destined to be one disappointment after another."

The king ordered his guards to bind the goatherd's feet with chains of iron, and cast him into the sea.

"Who was it, dear?" asked the queen, after the goatherd had been dragged away kicking with all of his might.

"That horrid goatherd, who says he's in love with Claire."

"Where is he going?"

"To the bottom of the sea."

"I suppose that's best, but do you think it's possible the girl may need love?"

"I should say not. Where on earth did you get that idea?"

"From a book."

"A book? How odd. Who wrote it?"

"A man named Smith."

"Is this Smith a king?"

"No."

"A prince?"

"I don't think so."

"A duke, possibly?"

"No, not a duke."

"Then throw the thing in the fire. What on earth can Smith have to do with us? Love indeed! There's nothing more dangerous in the world. You remember what happened to my older brother, don't you? He fell in love with some young lady, and the next thing you know, he was fighting a dragon who was in love with her, too. Or wanted to eat her, I don't recall. At any rate, the poor chap was burnt to a crisp."

"And as a result, you became king."

"Well, yes, I see your point. Perhaps love does have its place. But for others, dearest, not for us. Just imagine if we started loving Claire, and before we knew it a dragon was breathing fire on us. How would you like that?"

"But it's cheap, dear, and the royal treasury isn't as full as it used to be."

The king stroked his beard.

"I've got it. We'll raise the taxes."

"Again? What if there's a revolt?"

"It's safer than love," he said.

* * *

The king's soldiers loaded the goatherd onto a boat, and they sailed to the middle of the sea. When they reached their destination, they threw him over the side. The iron chains that bound his legs were heavy, and the goatherd sunk to the bottom.

He held his breath as he plunged downward. He passed schools of silvery herring that moved through the water like ghosts. Squids with waving tentacles stared at him through unblinking eyes. When he reached the bottom, he landed on white sand that had been sculpted into ripples by the waves. Red and yellow corals grew on large rocks scattered over the sandy floor. It was truly a lovely sight. And yet, despite the beauty that was all around him, the goatherd felt sad because the princess was far away, and he didn't have any air to breathe.

"This is a sticky situation," he thought. "But the dungeon and the desert looked bad, too, and I'm still alive. Who knows what the future may bring?"

So the goatherd swam with all his might. He rose up off the bottom of the sea, but the chains on his legs were so heavy that he couldn't get more than a few yards before he was pulled back down again. He yanked at the chains, but he couldn't get them off. Now his lungs started to burn, and his chest heaved with the urge to breathe.

"I cannot last much longer," he thought. "It's a shame that I must drown. I would have been so happy with the princess."

Then he remembered the moon dust the cat had given him, and he removed the pouch from his pocket. There wasn't much left, but the goatherd thought that if he could grow a castle here at the bottom of the sea, he could climb it to the surface. Or maybe instead of diamonds and rubies, one of the rooms would be filled with air, which at that moment was of greater value to him than all the jewels in the world.

Taking a pinch out of the leather pouch, he released it into the water. It sparkled as it floated away, but nothing happened. In desperation, the goatherd took the last remaining grains of moon dust, shoved them into his mouth, and swallowed.

He took in great deal of sea water, which was far too

salty for the his taste, but as soon as the moon dust got down his throat, his desire to breathe vanished. He was as comfortable down there on the bottom of the sea as any fish who didn't even know such a thing as land existed. The iron chains slipped off his feet, and he glided through the water, like a beam of light.

He traveled for miles, not knowing where he went, or why. He didn't wonder or care. He moved through the water, guided only by fate. At last his head broke through the waves, and water streamed from his hair. Overhead, a million stars were scattered across the dark sky. In front of him a darker mass blocked out the stars just above the horizon, and the goatherd thought that it must be an island. He took a deep breath—the first he had taken in hours—and swam toward it with strong strokes.

The island was rocky and bare, and as the goatherd climbed out of the water, lightening flashed in the distance. Far away, thunder rumbled, and a warm wind blew through the night. The goatherd stood still, breathing the air of the storm.

Out of the darkness a figure approached him. It was a lady dressed in a gown the color of the green sea. Her long hair reached down to her waist, and she walked with bare feet over the wave-washed rocks. On her hand was a ring with a jewel that was small, but wonderful to see. It was never the same for two moments in a row. It shifted among a thousand shades of blue and green, sparkling brightly for a moment or two, then becoming dark and somber, before it flashed with fire again. The lady took the ring from her hand, and slid it onto the goatherd's finger.

The wind blew stronger, and the lady's hair flew around the goatherd's face. He was lifted off his feet, and whirled through the air. Far below him he saw forests, plowed fields, and the cobbled streets of cities and towns. In the distance he could see his castle approaching as fast as the storm-chased wind. The goatherd flew through an open widow, and landed warm and dry under the covers of his bed.

* * *

"Father," said the princess, as she and the king drove through the countryside in the new royal carriage, "who is that young man walking by the river with his friends? Never before have I seen such a noble-looking person, and yet he seems familiar. Surely, it is not one of the princes who visited the palace?"

"Of course not," answered the king. "Your eyes play tricks on you. There is no one there but group of wretched peasants."

The king sighed.

"Young people have the most tiresome notions. No one knows what your mother and I endure. Now I must buy myself a pair of diamond-studded riding spurs in order to regain my peace of mind."

The king was going to say more on this subject, but the princess took her umbrella, and smashed it over the top of his head.

"Now you must buy me a new umbrella, and learn to be more polite to members of your family," she said.

The king had a headache all evening, and in the morning he summoned the Royal Scholars to advise him what to do.

They spoke together in conference, and then the Chief Scholar said,

"The royal visitors who have acquainted themselves with the princess represent only a small fraction of those individuals who, strictly from the point of view of nature, might reasonably qualify as potential suitors. If we increase the sample size, expanding the pool of candidates by one standard deviation, we would have a greater likelihood of success. In short, if the kings and princes won't marry her, maybe somebody else might."

The king reluctantly agreed, and put forth a proclamation that anyone of decent birth might come to the palace, and claim the hand of his daughter.

No one did.

"Now what?" asked the king.

"The legislative powers invested in the ruler of a state are often brought to bear in cases of need. Thus, when the crown lacks suitable resources, the subjects must be compelled to supply the necessary article."

So the king passed a law making it a crime not to fall in love with his daughter. The punishment for violating the law was death. The next day the kingdom was empty. Everyone had packed up and gone. The only one left was the goatherd.

The king glared at the Chief Scholar, who knit his

eyebrows, pulled his chin, and said, "Ahhhh, an unexpected development, to be sure."

Then the scholar had a thought.

"I believe I have it," he said. "The simple rules of logic tell us that when all possible solutions but one have been eliminated, that which remains must be correct."

Since the goatherd was the only one left, he would have to marry the princess. She was brought into the throne room, and everything was explained to her.

"So you see, my dear," said the king, "the logic is inescapable. I don't say it's what I had hoped for, but the consolation is that your mother and I will be rid of you at last. The goatherd is a villain, and the worst of it is that he loves you, but I'm sure you will put an end to that without the slightest effort on your part.

A letter was sent to the goatherd communicating the news. He wrote back saying that he would marry the princess under two conditions. The first was that the king had to give back all the land he had taken from the nobles. The second was that the law had be changed so that everybody could come back, as long as they promised NOT to fall in love with the princess. The king agreed. His subjects considered the new law to be easy and agreeable, and everyone came back.

After returning all the land as he had promised, the king found that the royal treasury was empty. The princess could be given no dowry at all, and would have to go to the goatherd with nothing but her own self.

"He will be here soon," said the king the next morning.

"I hope you like him."

The princess went outside, and looked down the palace drive. She saw a young man walking toward her. As he came closer, she recognized the boy she had saved many years ago. He was older now, and was grown handsome and strong.

He walked up to her, and said, "Good morning, Princess. I have loved you since the day we first met. Will you marry me?"

Whatever her faults may have been, the princess was a realist.

"I didn't expect to be quite this poor," she said. "However, if I cannot have carriages, dresses, or jewels, perhaps it won't be so bad, if at least I have love."

The goatherd laughed, and his smile was as warm as the sun-drenched desert. The princess moved closer, and saw that his eyes sparkled with the colors of the evening sea, and were deeper than any buried vault. They were very close now, so the princess made a place for herself within his arms, and decided that she was probably right.

THE DARK FOREST

Part 1

It was just before dawn, and Prince Cor, the eldest son of the King of the Fairies, stood at the edge of the Dark Forest. The guides his father had sent with him were asleep in their beds, and Cor imagined how angry his father would be if he knew the risk Cor was taking. But he had found himself awake while it was still dark, and he was too excited to wait for the others to get up.

Cor had dressed quietly, and slipped away, out into the cool air. The sky was dark, but the air was full of the smells of morning.

Cor was on his way to join the valiant fairy knights who lived in the Dark Forest, and battled the evil beasts that haunted the woods. The beasts hated the fairies, and their only desire was to destroy them. The fairy knights protected the kingdom, and they were said to be fearless.

"I will be fearless like them," thought Cor.

And so, Cor had sneaked away from those who were to bring him in safety to the fortress of the fairy knights. He planned to enter the Dark Forest alone.

A cold wind blew from the woods. It swept across Cor's face, and made his heart beat fast. His head jerked up, and his eyes scanned the woods in front of him. This was not the wind he had expected. Winds and breezes are the fairies' friends, and fairies recognize the winds the way people recognize the faces of their neighbors. Cor had expected a fresh wind with the promise of dawn. It should have been a playful wind, with the farewell wishes of the night, and the happy scent of the earth waking from its slumbers. But this was a wind he had never met before. It was a dead wind that carried no tales of the living world.

The trees tossed their branches. The joy of being on his own disappeared, and all of a sudden Cor's legs twitched with the desire to run. This nameless wind that stretched out its arms from the forest did not belong to the world Cor knew. He wondered why his father allowed this wind to roam his kingdom. But his father was far away, and Cor said to himself,

"I am the eldest son of the King of the Fairies. My father rules this land. I will go and see what causes this wind to blow. And if I can, I will do something."

Holding tight to the hilt of his sword, Cor entered the

woods.

He followed a forest path until he came to a small village. There was a handful of houses, but they were unlike the places where fairies usually live. Fairies never let their homes fall into disrepair. Like the forest itself, fairies love harmony, but these homes were ruined. Cor approached the nearest one. The moss on the roof was brown, the windows were all broken, and the door had been ripped off its hinges.

Cor shivered. Where were the fairies who lived here? His eyes traveled from one home to the next, when suddenly the ground shook, and before Cor realized what was happening, a giant creature burst from among the trees.

It moved with hideous speed. One moment Cor was alone, and the next there was a blur of claws and teeth. Cor was knocked down by the force of the attack, but he hit the ground rolling, and in an instant he was on his feet with his sword drawn. The creature crouched in front of him, motionless. It hadn't expected an armed opponent.

The beast was covered with black hair like a spider. Its powerful hind legs were long, so that its knees rose above the rest of its body. Its front legs were short, and its head stuck out almost even with the ground. It had the ears of a bat, and its mouth was full of jagged teeth. It was twice the size of Cor.

"I must fight this creature," thought Cor.

But he could not. Fear robbed him of all control over his arms and legs. The creature kept its eyes on Cor's sword, then leaped forward, slashing with its claws. Cor closed his eyes, and swung. The creature shrieked in pain, there was a swish of air, and it was gone.

Cor stood still, breathing hard. Would the beast attack again? Would there be others with it next time? There was a rustling in the bushes behind him. Cor spun around, and stretched out his sword to meet the heavy blow of the beast.

But the collision never came. In front of him stood three fairies. Their faces were stern.

"Are you hurt?" asked one of the fairies.

Cor looked down. His jacket was torn, and his body ached, but otherwise he was uninjured.

"No. Its claws missed their mark. What was it?"

"It was a Staggart. They're fast, but they're cowards. They never stand and fight. To kill one of them, you must lie in ambush, and take it by surprise."

"Do you hunt them?" asked Cor.

"Yes. We hunt all the dark beasts."

"Then you must be fairy knights. My name is Cor. I've come to join you."

"Why are you alone?"

"I woke early," said Cor. "I didn't want to bother the others who were with me. I thought I would go on my own to see what the forest held."

The fairy knight frowned. "Never do that again," he said.

They walked together through the woods, and late in the afternoon they arrived at the fortress. It was a low building made from hard-packed earth. Inside were tunnels that extended deep into the ground, and it was in these tunnels that the fairies lived. The fortress was surrounded by a high wall made of oak planks. Walkways, which were patrolled day and night, ran along the top of the wall.

Cor entered the fortress through a narrow gate. Guards stood on either side, and saluted the lieutenant who came out to meet them. Cor and the fairy knights entered the main building, and walked down a sloping passage.

The hallways were lit by torches that flickered with orange flames, and stained the walls with their black smoke. The smell of burning oil made Cor wrinkle his nose. They passed though narrow rooms lined with bunks, where Cor saw armor hanging from the foot of each bunk. Some of the armor was made of leather, some of light chain mail.

They entered the mess hall where the fairies ate their meals. Hard, wooden benches flanked long tables. At one of these benches sat two fairies, speaking together with their heads bent over a map that lay between them. Cor was brought forward, and one of the fairies stood up to shake his hand.

"Welcome, Prince," he said. "My name is Regador. Your father did me the honor of appointing me commander of this fortress."

"My father has spoken of you often," said Cor. "He told me stories of your bravery, and he hopes I will learn from you."

Regador was short with broad shoulders. His face bore scars from the battles he had fought against the dark beasts. Cor's eyes lingered on the scars.

"They are the trophies of my mistakes, young Prince," said Regador with a wink. "Each is more precious to me than all my victories rolled into one."

Cor's first task was to learn how to fight as a member of a team of fairy knights. He was given a book that described their strategies and maneuvers, and was told to memorize every page. Regador quizzed him, and made him recite each maneuver until it came without thought. One night Regador shook Cor from a deep sleep, and placed pen and paper in his hands.

"Copy as much of the book as you can remember," Regador said.

The room was dark. Cor was given neither candle nor lamp, but before the sun was up, a perfect copy of the book lay on Cor's desk.

The next day Cor was allowed to join the exercises with the other fairy knights. They drilled for hours until the knowledge of their fighting maneuvers settled in their muscles and their swords.

"When the time comes to fight, you will be afraid, and you may find yourself unable to think clearly," said Regador, as he swung his sword at Cor, trying to penetrate his defense. "Your arms and legs must act on their own, and the only way that can be achieved is with practice."

"I will do all you tell me," said Cor, moving his sword quickly to block each of Regador's attacks. "But I do not think I will be afraid."

Regador lowered his sword.

"Trust me," he said, "you will be afraid."

Each night, while the others slept, one of the fairies walked the walls that surrounded the fortress. After a month of training, Cor was allowed to serve his first night as watch. He was told to wake the others if anything happened.

Cor paced the walkway that ran across the top of wall, remembering his encounter with the Staggart. He had put the beast to flight, but why did his body freeze when he had looked into its eyes?

He tried to remember everything his father had taught him about the beasts. They were unlike all the other creatures of the forest, and no one could tell Cor where they came from. Legend had it that the dark beasts appeared ages ago, when the fairies first emerged from the forest. His father understood the beasts better than anyone else, but he rarely spoke about their origin.

"Those who fight them will learn where they came from," was all he would say.

His father had been a fairy knight when he was young, and he had taught Cor about the life of a soldier. He spoke about hardship and about death. Fairies do not grow old and die like humans, but some will fall in battle, and when that happens their spirits are returned to the forest. Sometimes a fairy's spirit will make its home in a flower and sometimes in a tree. Very rarely, a fairy's spirit will visit a human child, and when that happens, the child is marked with the sign of the fairies.

The king had tried to persuade Cor to give up his wish to become a knight.

"There are dangers you don't understand," he said. "It

would be better for you to stay here in the palace, and find some other way to serve our people."

"What dangers?" asked Cor. "Tell me what they are, and I will be prepared."

The king hesitated. Then he said, "Of all things, beware the conquered enemy. The enemy you believe defeated is the most deadly, especially when it is inside you."

"I don't understand," said Cor.

"The most fearsome of all the beasts is the Dualag. It can take any shape, but its true form is that of a serpent. Its tail carries a poisonous sting with the power to turn a fairy against himself. The poison divides the soul, and plants a seed of darkness. It blinds the fairy, so that he cannot tell his true self from the rising evil."

"I will be careful, and I will never let down my guard," Cor had promised his father.

The night was dark, and Cor walked the wall with deliberate steps. He glanced from side to side, his eyes trying to pierce the darkness.

"This world belongs to the beasts," he thought, and he wondered how long it would be before the sun rose to make the earth familiar again.

He squinted his eyes, but he could see only a short distance into the forest. He heard frogs croaking, and the wind rustling in the trees. These were sounds he had heard all his life, but tonight they sounded menacing. Was the tone different? Was the rhythm different?

"It's only my ears playing tricks on me," he thought.

Then he wondered, "Am I afraid?"

His heart beat fast, and again he tried to discover what was different about the sounds. But he could find no solution.

"They're the same! I have to stop this, or I'll drive myself crazy."

But Cor couldn't persuade himself that they were the same, and his ears strained to find the hidden clue.

Then he heard something definite. From a clump of bushes in the woods came the crunching sound of something heavy. Cor stopped and listened. He listened for a long time, but the sound wasn't repeated, and he wondered if he had imagined it.

"Should I wake the others?" he thought.

Cor had been told, "Wake us if anything happens." But he didn't know if the sound he heard, or maybe thought he heard, counted as "anything." He realized "anything" could mean something big or something small, and now he wished he had asked more questions about when to sound the alarm.

"I'll go have a look," he thought.

Cor knew that he could move through the forest in silence. He had always been better at that than anyone he knew.

"At least I'll learn something before I wake the others."

He placed his hands on the railing that ran along the top of the wall, pulled himself up, and dropped lightly to the ground on the other side. He advanced through the forest, as silent as the trees.

After taking a dozen steps into the darkness, Cor stopped. He saw something, just ahead of him. It blended in with the forest, and it was hard for him to make out the details. He moved closer, and crouched down behind a clump of bushes, his thoughts wholly concentrated on the shadowy figure ahead of him.

A click snapped the silence of the forest.

Cor stood still, and held his breath. He had been careless, and stepped on a twig. For a long time nothing happened, then the thing turned its head, and looked in Cor's direction. It jumped into the air, leaped past Cor, and ran away into the woods. It was only a deer. Cor took a deep breath, and relaxed. He felt like laughing. It was nothing.

And then the forest crashed with the sound of ripping branches, and a Necrofang appeared, roaring in the darkness.

The Necrofang was huge—as big as a dozen fairy knights. It was covered with black fur, and had horns that extended forward from either side of its head. Worst of all were its eyes. They glowed yellow with hatred. The terrible eyes found Cor, and held him in a grip of fear until he was unable to move. The Necrofang lowered its head, and charged.

Cor felt the ground tremble as massive hooves pounded the forest floor. Dirt and leaves flew into the air. The nostrils of the beast flared, as it prepared to drive its horns through Cor's body. Somewhere in the back of Cor's mind was the thought that he should draw his sword, but the burning yellow eyes held him firm, and he stood paralyzed.

A hand grasped Cor's arm, and pulled. He tripped over his feet, and fell face first to the ground. The Necrofang thundered by, and Cor, blinking the dirt from his eyes, saw Regador standing above him. Fairy knights sleep lightly, and Regador had been restless knowing it was Cor's first night on watch. When he had found that Cor was not at his post, Regador had gathered a band of fairies, and they had gone out in search of the missing prince.

Cor could move again, and he got back on his feet. The fairies formed a protective circle around him, facing outward with swords drawn. There were other beasts now, and all Cor could see was a confused jumble of teeth, horns, hoofs, and charging bodies. The beasts were larger and stronger than the fairies, but the fairies struck with precision. The air was filled with the cries of the beasts, as the points of the swords found their targets.

They fought their way back to the safety of the fortress, moving like dancers in a ballet. Strike, withdraw, strike, withdraw. The fury that drove the beasts was no match for the fairies' practiced maneuvers. Soon they were inside the fortress walls. The armor of the fairy knights was stained with blood, but it was the blood of the beasts. None of the fairies had been hurt.

Later, as they cleaned their armor, Cor turned to Regador, and said, "That wasn't how I expected my first battle to be. I was a coward."

"The first battle is never as one expects, but you weren't a coward," said Regador. "You stayed with us, and allowed us to protect you. None of us was hurt, and no one can ask for more than that."

"Why did we run from the beasts? Isn't it our duty to fight them?" asked Cor.

"We didn't run, we retreated. There's a difference. A retreat is an orderly maneuver of battle, and we fought well. We gained the safety of the fortress, we inflicted injuries on the beasts, and I think some of them will die from their wounds. A well executed retreat can be more deadly than an attack. We've earned the right to be satisfied with our work tonight. But why were you outside the fortress? Why weren't you at your post?"

"I heard something, and I went to investigate."

"That wasn't the job you were assigned. Your place was on the wall, standing guard."

"I thought I could move silently through the trees, and return with valuable information."

"We work together, Cor. All your talents will be put to use, but if you act on your own, you'll place yourself and others in danger. When you serve as night sentry, your place is on the wall. You must wake me if you think something needs to be investigated."

"I will do better next time," said Cor.

"Our job is to protect your father's kingdom, and to survive," said Regador. "There is no one here to impress."

"I tell you I will do better next time," said Cor. "You will see."

* * *

Cor trained hard, and learned as much as he could about the beasts. As he practiced his maneuvers, he tried to imagine the charging bulk of the Necrofang with its burning eyes of yellow hatred.

He was quick with his sword, and had a keen eye that allowed him find the weakness of an opponent's defense. He became more and more skilled, and even those who were most experienced found it hard to keep up with him. Cor dreamed of someday being the best of all the fairy knights.

Cor took his turn as watch, and persuaded some of the others to give him their turns as well. He paced the walls night after night, staring into the darkness. But it was a time when the beasts waited, and Cor became impatient.

He said to Regador one day, "Why don't we organize an attack? I'm ready to put what I've learned to good use."

Regador shook his head.

"Don't be anxious to seek out evil. The battle will come. When it does, if you fight well, you'll prevail, and be better prepared to fight again. Your courage will turn the evil into good. But now is the time to train and rest. Make the most of it. The beasts are out there, and we will have to meet them. But it's unwise to look for danger, when there is no need."

The need came soon. A Baubas was sighted near a village not far from the fairies' stronghold. Five knights would be sent to protect the village, and Regador chose Cor to be one of the five. They were led by an older knight named Fyddon.

The band of fairy knights traveled through the forest looking for signs of the Baubas. Cor remembered what he had learned about the Baubas. It was fast and strong, but it fought alone. It was so full of malice that any other creature, even one of its own kind, filled it with fury.

They arrived at the village, and Cor's stomach tightened as he saw the fear in the faces of the fairies who lived there. The village fairies told the knights everything they knew about the Baubas. They believed it was somewhere nearby, but when the knights searched the surrounding area, they didn't find the usual signs of a Baubas moving through the woods.

Cor and the others remained in the village, and after a while, the fear faded from the villagers' faces. The fairy knights began to wonder if the Baubas had moved on, and whether it was time for them to leave.

"It hasn't left," said Cor. "It's waiting."

"How can you be sure?" asked Fyddon.

Cor shook his head. He didn't know.

Cor persuaded Fyddon to search for the Baubas deeper within the forest. They walked together along a path where the trees grew close together. Rotting plants crowded out the undergrowth, their rank smell overpowering the other scents of the forest. After a while, the two fairies came to a place where the path divided, and Cor looked at Fyddon.

"You decide," said Fyddon.

Without hesitating, Cor turned to the left. As they moved forward, his feeling of unease grew.

"How do I know it's near?" he thought.

Cor wondered if his father had sensed the presence of the beasts when he had fought as a fairy knight. The trees rustled in the wind. Everything sounded like it always did, but Cor's ears again strained to discover something that disturbed him. But as it had been on the night when he paced the fortress walls, he couldn't tell what it was that made his heart beat fast. Cor looked at Fyddon, and Fyddon drew his sword. They left the forest trail, and moved toward a clump of twisted trees that lay some distance away.

As they came closer, they saw branches on the ground that had been ripped from the trees. They saw deep gashes in the bark. And then the monster was upon them.

Cor knew that the Baubas would be strong, but he was unprepared for the ferocity of its attack. The Baubas towered above the two fairies and used the weight of its massive body to drive them deeper into the woods. Their feet caught in tangled vines, and whip-like branches blinded their eyes.

Cor and Fyddon stood shoulder to shoulder so they could double the effect of their sword work. But the Baubas was fast, and it parried their attacks with its claws. The swords of the fairies waved harmlessly in the air. Cor looked into the eyes of the beast, hesitated, then drew back, leaving Fyddon to fight the enemy as best he could.

But Fyddon was overmatched. He gave ground as he avoided the deadly swipe of the claws, and little by little, the

Baubas drove Fyddon backwards. Cor followed, just out of reach of the beast's fury.

Fyddon's sword began to slow. His feet slipped on the uneven ground, and Cor knew that the end of the battle was near. Soon the Baubas would deliver the final blow that would crush the exhausted fairy knight.

The Baubas reared upward, lifted its giant leg high above its head, and Cor saw his chance. He ran forward, and slipped his sword beneath the raised forelimb. The blade penetrated the beast's hide, found the gap between its ribs, and entered its heart. With a choking sound, the Baubas fell to the ground.

Fyddon crouched with his hands on his knees, breathing fast.

"Well done!" he said. "Where did you learn that?"

"I guessed at what it would do," said Cor.

"You guessed right. Your instinct is good, like your father's was when he was a knight. It's a lucky thing. All of the Baubas are large, but this one was the biggest I've ever seen. There was a moment when I thought we would fail. We must teach your strategy to the others."

They walked back to the village to tell of their success, and for the first time in weeks, Cor breathed freely.

* * *

In the days and months that followed, Cor's reputation as a resourceful fighter increased. He learned the rhythm of attack and retreat, and fought well against the beasts who drove themselves onto the defenses of the fairy stronghold. He learned to work with the other fairies to confuse, separate, and overcome the beasts. He fought the Baalberith, whose horns were made of gold; the Gresil, that fouled the waters where fairies went to drink; and the Renwie, the most clever of all the beasts.

Cor was known best for his ability to track the beasts. His instinct rarely led him wrong. He sensed what they would do, and Cor believed there was not a single beast in all the forest that was a match for his skill. But he had not yet faced another Necrofang.

The weather turned cold with the coming of winter, and soon the snow began to fall. The fairies spent their time strengthening their defenses, repairing the damage that had been done to the walls of the fortress, and making sure they were well supplied with firewood. Winter was not a time for fighting. The confusion of the drifting snow favored the attacks of the beasts.

Soon, however, a report reached the fortress of a Staggart near the river Koi. The fairies who fished the river begged the knights to send them help. Cor volunteered to go, and said he would take Fletcher with him. Fletcher had recently joined the fairy knights, and Cor had undertaken the task of training him. Fletcher hadn't experienced battle yet, but he was eager. When he was not practicing maneuvers, he spent his time polishing his armor, and sharpening his sword.

Regador was reluctant to send two inexperienced fairies on a mission in winter that would take them so far from the fortress, but Cor's confidence won him over. After all, it was only a Staggart. The two young fairies set off on their journey early the next morning.

Snow was everywhere, and the paths of the forest were difficult to follow. The whole world was covered in a blanket of white. The rounded piles sparkled in the sunlight, making the forest strangely beautiful. Fletcher walked along, talking cheerfully, and enjoying the fresh smells that quickened his blood.

Cor spoke little. He was concentrating on their surroundings. Familiar landmarks were hard to recognize, and Cor knew that the covering blanket of snow would make it easy for them to lose their way. Places of safety and places of danger were hard to tell apart, and he understood why the fairies didn't like to fight in winter.

Cor was a good woodsman, though, and they reached the river in safety. They walked along its banks until they came to the village where the river fairies lived.

The village consisted of a small group of cottages that stood near the water. Piers where the fisher-fairies moored their boats extended out into the river. Gray nets lay piled near the boats, and spiky fishing poles stuck up into the air.

The fairies of the fishing village welcomed the knights, and showed them the cottages that had been destroyed by the Staggart. The fairies who had lost their homes had escaped without harm, but they were afraid. Fletcher avoided their eyes.

Later that night, Cor said to Fletcher, "Tomorrow we will hunt the Staggart. If we're lucky, we'll find it, and slay it with little danger to ourselves."

"I'm not afraid of danger, Prince," said Fletcher. "I'm only afraid of not fighting well."

"Just follow my instructions," said Cor. "The Staggart will be good for your first encounter."

The next morning Cor and Fletcher visited the places where signs of the Staggart's passing had been seen. Cor went down on his hands and knees to examine the torn branches and trampled bushes. Unease began to prick at the inside of his stomach. The more signs he saw, the more the unease became a growing fear. The beast they tracked was larger and more fierce than a Staggart. Cor sensed a cold hatred. But he wasn't sure yet, so he kept his doubts to himself.

"Look, Prince," said Fletcher, pointing to a clump of trampled bushes. "These bend to the south, while the others bend to the north. It looks as if the Staggart came this way twice. Do you think it knows we are following it, and is trying to circle back behind us?"

"It may be," said Cor.

"Are Staggarts so clever? I've heard they're quick, but I didn't know they used strategy."

"Staggarts usually don't."

"What might it be? If it's a clever, more dangerous beast it will bring us greater glory, won't it?"

"First, let's see if we can get back to the fortress alive, and then we'll think about glory. There are only two of us, Fletcher. We came to fight a Staggart, not some unknown beast."

"Will you give up the hunt, Prince? What about the fairies who live by the river? Will we abandon them? If we return to the fortress to get help, it may be too late by the time we return."

Cor hesitated. "We could send a messenger back to the fortress, and remain to protect the village as best we can," said Cor in a quiet voice, as if thinking out loud.

Cor looked down at the bushes that bent in opposite directions. He remembered how he had been mastered by fear the night he stood watch on the fortress wall, and he clenched his fists.

"No," he said at last. "It would be too dangerous to send one of the villagers at this time of year. You and I, Fletcher, we will hunt this beast, and we will kill it."

They continued to follow the tracks, which became more and more confused. It was clear now that the beast knew it was being followed. They tracked it all day, until the sun was low in the sky, and the light began to fade.

"Will we continue tomorrow?" asked Fletcher.

Cor looked up from the ground where his eyes had been straining to unravel the mystery of the tracks.

"I didn't know it was so late," he said. "You're right. It's time to go back to the village."

Cor straightened his back, and rubbed his eyes with his fists. It was a relief to take his mind off the confusion of the tracks. He heard Fletcher gasp. Cor looked up, and his gaze met a pair of yellow eyes. The earth shook as the giant creature tore the ground beneath its hooves, and now the truth forced itself upon Cor. He should have known it before: it was a Necrofang that stalked the river fairies—and two knights, no matter how skilled, were no match for this beast.

Cor and Fletcher dove out of the path of the charging Necrofang, and drew their swords. The beast roared, and renewed its attack. Cor knew that if they tried to run, the Necrofang would drive its horns into their backs. Their only hope was to stand and fight.

The Necrofang charged again, and Cor thought, "Are Fletcher and I to be killed today? If I can, I will save him."

He ordered Fletcher to stand aside while Cor remained in front of the Necrofang, drawing the attack upon himself. Each time the beast charged, Cor leaped away, rolling on the ground, while Fletcher stepped forward to attack from the side. But the Necrofang moved fast, giving Fletcher little time to advance, and his sword couldn't penetrate the thick hide of the beast

The fairies fought bravely, but in the end they couldn't resist the overwhelming strength of the Necrofang. Cor pulled himself to his feet for what felt like the hundredth time. His arms and legs ached. He wondered what it would feel like to die.

"I'm not afraid," he thought, trying to catch his breath. "At least I can say that."

Then he imagined the beast turning on Fletcher, and that was more than he could bear.

"If the end is to come, let it come now," he thought.

The Necrofang prepared for another attack, and Cor held his sword with both hands, his arms straight out in front of him, his elbows locked. Cor hoped that when the collision came, the force of the Necrofang's own weight would drive Cor's blade deep enough to wound it. That might give Fletcher a chance to escape.

The Necrofang charged, and Cor ran forward to meet it. His exhausted legs dragged across the uneven ground, and after taking a only few steps, he tripped on a vine, and fell. The Necrofang's hooves pounded toward him. But before the beast could trample the fallen fairy knight, Fletcher ran out from the safety of his cover, his face pale, and now it was he who held his sword out in front of him. He stood over Cor, guarding him from the Necrofang, and when the collision came, he was thrown into the air. His body crashed into a tree, fell to the ground, and lay there in a heap.

All was not lost, however. Fletcher's sword had done its work. The Necrofang roared with pain, and blood poured from a wound in its shoulder. Cor was on his feet again now. He scooped up Fletcher in his arms, and summoned the strength to run. The Necrofang tried to follow, but the wound slowed its pace. It began to limp, and at last it stopped, watching the fleeing fairies with its yellow eyes.

Cor ran through the evening twilight with Fletcher in his arms, hoping to reach help in time to save his friend.

When they arrived at the village, Fletcher was laid on a bed, and examined by an old fairy who brought a basket of dried leaves and clay pots filled with ointments. She removed Fletcher's armor, exposing a deep wound made by the Necrofang's horn. The old fairy covered the wound with pungent herbs, then wrapped bandages around

Fletcher's chest. Every morning she came to remove the bandages, place herbs on the wound, and wrap fresh strips of cloth around his chest. But the wound didn't close, and each day Fletcher became thinner and weaker.

He drifted in and out of sleep, waking occasionally to see Cor sitting by his side. One evening, after he had slept most of the day, Fletcher said to Cor,

"I had the strangest dream. I saw a girl sitting all alone. She must have been sad, or maybe lonely, because she was crying. I watched her tears drop to the ground, and in the place where they fell, a flower appeared."

Fletcher paused, gathering his strength, before going on with his dream.

"The girl was so surprised that she stopped crying. She took the flower in her hand, and held it up to her face. And then I saw that the sadness was gone, and in its place was joy."

Fletcher looked up at his friend.

"It was me, Prince. I was the flower she held."

Fletcher's eyes lit up, and his thin face relaxed into a smile. Then his eyes closed, and the light was gone.

* * *

The next morning the forest was hidden by a blanket of fog. It was warm, and the ground was soaked with melted snow. Cor stepped carefully in order to avoid leaving footprints in the mud. He was alone, and he was on the track of the Necrofang.

He knew that it was close, moving away from him, but its progress was slow. Cor quickened his steps.

Then he saw it on the forest path ahead of him, limping on its injured leg. As Cor drew near, the Necrofang turned. It growled, and bared its teeth. Its eyes fixed on Cor, the smoldering flames intensified by the pain in its leg. Cor returned its stare. The forest fell silent.

Cor held the gaze of the yellow eyes with his own. Here was the thing that had killed his friend. In the intensity of Cor's hatred, he was calm.

The Necrofang didn't attack. As it stared at Cor, its yellow eyes flickered, and it took a halting step backward. The fairy knight walked forward, and plunged his sword into the Necrofang's heart.

"Let the beasts of the forest fear me," he whispered as he pulled out the blade. "For I will avenge upon them the death of my friend."

Cor wiped his sword clean, and walked deeper into the woods.

He walked for hours. He knew he should return to the fortress, but he wouldn't go yet. The well-ordered stratagems of the fairy knights had no appeal for him today. He had killed a Necrofang, and he was the scourge of the beasts. He walked deeper into the woods.

It was late morning, and the sun had burned the fog away when Cor came upon a track deep within the forest. It was a track he had never seen before. Sometimes he thought he recognized it, and at other times it looked strange. Doubt crept into Cor's mind. This was a beast that would fight in unfamiliar ways. The discipline of the fairy knights no longer seemed so dull, and he wished he had someone by his side.

"I'm a better warrior than I was before," he thought. "I faced a Necrofang alone, and I killed it. I don't think a fairy knight has ever done that before. But now it's time to go back to the fortress, and tell the others what happened."

Cor chose a path that led in the direction of the fortress, but now he found that he couldn't escape the strange track. Each turn he took, thinking it would carry him away from this mysterious beast, uncovered new signs of its presence. What magic did this beast possess that enabled it to entangle a fairy in its track?

Soon however, Cor became confident that he was moving in the right direction. The ground was firmer under his feet, and the footpath wasn't as clogged with vines. It was when beams of light first pierced the tree tops, and Cor believed he had found his way to safety, that the beast attacked.

Cor struggled to draw his sword as the thing rushed upon him. It was covered with fur like a Necrofang, but it was smaller, faster, and more agile. Its body was long, like the body of a weasel, and it ran on eight short legs that moved faster than Cor's eyes could follow.

The beast's jaws snapped at Cor, forcing him backward, away from the light, back into the darkness where the ground was soft, and the trees crowded in on one another.

Cor circled around, placing his back to the open part of the forest where he could fight more freely. He was using his sword well now, and succeeded in drawing blood on two occasions. The beast pulled its lips back from its mouth, exposing row upon row of short, pointed teeth. It hissed, and attacked with renewed fury.

Again and again the point of Cor's sword cut the beast's hide, maddening it with pain. Its anger made it careless, and Cor forced it into a clearing where the sun shone bright. The beast fought with its eyes squinted, blinded by the winter sun. It could no longer keep up with the rapid motion of Cor's sword, and with a final, sure thrust, the battle was over. The beast lay at Cor's feet, and Cor was wiping the edge of his sword on a patch of grass.

"I was lucky today," thought Cor. "It was foolish to hunt alone so deep within the woods. I'm going back to the others, and from now on I'll be more careful."

There was a sound behind him. The beast still moved, scraping its body along the ground. Its chest expanded as it took a breath. It breathed again, and yet again, inflating like a balloon. Its fur became rough, and the claws on its feet grew longer. Four of its legs pulled up and disappeared into its body, and the remaining four grew thick like tree trunks. It rose to its feet, let out a hideous roar, and threw itself upon the fairy knight.

This time, the battle went in the beast's favor. Try as he might, Cor could not keep to the open areas of the forest, and the beast drove him back into the darkness. Cor was tired, and his attacks were weak. His best hope was to stay out of reach of the sharp claws. His retreats came closer and closer together, and soon he and the beast were deep within the darkness of the woods.

The trees were so close together now that it became difficult for Cor to use his sword. At times he could only hold it straight out in front of him as a defense against the powerful lunges of his enemy. What was this thing? Cor wondered whether he could defeat this creature that did not die when wounded, and could change its shape at will. But Cor couldn't run away. With its powerful legs the beast would be on his back in an instant. He had to find another way of escape.

Cor couldn't keep his eyes on the beast, and look where he was going at the same time. As he backed away, his head crashed against a low branch. Pain shot through his skull, and the forest went blurry, but as he recovered, he had an idea.

He grabbed the branch that had struck his head, and pulled himself on to it. He scrambled upward branch by branch until he was high above the forest floor. The beast howled in fury as it watched its prey escape out of reach. It scraped its claws against the bark, but it couldn't climb.

Cor sat on a high limb, holding tight to the trunk of the tree. He was safe for now, but he wondered how long it would last. Would the beast stand guard below? What would happen when night came? How long could he stay awake? The powerful beast that clawed the tree trunk below him was something he had never seen before, and Cor realized that he knew less about the dark beasts than he had thought.

The scraping sound stopped, and a moment later the

beast was gone. The forest was quiet again except for the sound of the wind blowing through the branches of the trees. Cor shivered. His body was covered with sweat. Should he climb down, and try to escape, or was it a trick?

Suddenly, the tree shook. The beast had come back, running with its head lowered, crashing its skull into the trunk. There was a cracking sound, and the beast was gone. But once again it came charging back, and hit the tree like a battering ram. This time the cracking sound was louder, and the tree no longer stood straight. Cor held on tight to the branch. One more blow would bring the tree down.

Cor knew he had to get out. If the fall didn't kill him, a broken arm or leg would make it impossible to fight.

The trunk now tipped at a steep angle, and a branch from a neighboring tree was almost within reach. The beast charged for the final blow, and just before it collided into the trunk for the last time, Cor jumped.

The tree fell with the sound of crunching branches, but Cor was safe, clinging to the neighboring tree. His feet dangled above the ground. The beast plunged its front legs into the canopy of the fallen tree, then pulled back when it found no fairy knight. It stuck its nose into the branches, to see if anything was hiding inside.

Hand over hand, Cor moved along the branch until he hung directly above the beast. He held his breath. If it looked up and saw him, all would be lost. But the beast didn't look up. It pushed its nose deeper into the branches of the fallen tree.

Cor let go.

He landed on the back of the great beast, and with a roar, it reared up onto its hind legs, then took off through the forest.

It ran at a terrible speed, scraping against trees and branches, trying to knock Cor off. But Cor bent low, and flattened himself against the beast's hairy back.

With his left hand Cor gripped a handful of fur, and with his right he drew his sword. The ring of the sword scraping against the scabbard made the beast increase its speed, but it couldn't shake off the determined fairy knight. Cor reached around, and pulled the sharp blade deep across the hairy throat. The creature's legs buckled, and it fell to the ground

Cor rolled off its back, and lay by its side. Exhaustion covered him, and his sword dropped from his hand. He lay motionless except for the heaving of his chest.

Above him a bird perched on the limb of a tree. It tipped its head, as if surprised to see a fairy so deep within the forest. It tipped its head the other way, then suddenly it gave a screech, and the sound of clapping wings filled the air. Cor reached for his sword, and struggled to his feet. The beast had moved.

Its fur pulled into its skin, which became scaly and white. The body grew long, and its legs became shorter until they disappeared completely. The eyes, which were now slits, stared at Cor, and the beast slithered forward on its belly. It was a serpent, and now Cor knew the name of the enemy he fought. On its tail he saw the sting with the poison that divided a fairy's heart. It was the Dualag. Cor tore his gaze away from the serpent's eyes, and ran.

He stumbled on roots and vines as he plunged through the forest. Behind him was the sound of the serpent moving across the ground. Ahead of him he saw a patch of light. Cor wondered if he had found a clearing, or possibly the edge of the forest itself. He ran faster, but now the serpent was off to his side. If it managed to get ahead of him, he would be cut off, unable to escape the darkness of the woods.

Hope and fear banished the weakness from his legs. He changed course, and came up behind the serpent. The serpent's body made an arc as it turned to face Cor, and for a moment its side was exposed. Cor swung his sword, and green liquid oozed from the place where his sword cut.

The jaws of the serpent shot forward, and Cor jumped to the side to avoid a pair of fangs, each as long as his arm. The body of the serpent closed around him in a ring of scaly flesh.

Cor looked at the place where his sword had struck the side of the Dualag. He saw nothing there—no wound, not even a scar. The cut was gone. The long tube-like body of the serpent expanded and contracted as it breathed, and the circle that surrounded Cor closed in.

Cor jumped over the serpent's body, and once again ran toward the light. He had no plan now. He didn't know what would happen when he reached the edge of the woods. He only knew that he had to escape the darkness.

His breath burned his lungs, but his legs didn't slow down. At last he broke through the bushes at the edge of the forest. The light streamed down upon him, but Cor threw himself to the ground, and slid to a stop. He was inches from the edge of a precipice. Hundreds of feet below him flowed the river Koi. The clearing where he stood was nothing but a narrow shelf of rock, and now there was nowhere left to run.

The Dualag emerged from the trees. Its eyes were thin lines in the dazzling sunlight. The clearing was empty. No fairy knight could be seen. The Dualag's tongue flicked in and out, tasting the ground. It slithered back and forth across the precipice, until at last it reached the edge. It stuck its head out into the air, and looked down.

Just below the serpent's head stood Cor, balanced on a projection of rock. He gripped his sword with both hands, and swung. The sword passed through the Dualag's massive neck, and Cor saw the head tumble down to the valley below.

Cor climbed back up onto the precipice, keeping his eyes on the headless serpent. It didn't move. This was not a wound it would recover from. Cor removed his leather armor, and examined his bruise-covered body. He unbuckled his sword, and stretched out his arms.

The headless body of the Dualag lay on the edge of the cliff. Cor thought he could push it over the side with his foot, but he hesitated to touch it. The Dualag was fearsome even in death. Cor shrugged, and gave it a kick.

As his foot touched the serpent's body, it convulsed. The tail jumped off the ground, and Cor watched in horror, unable to move, as the black sting flew through the air.

With a hollow thump, the tail knocked him off his feet,

and the sting scraped across his chest. Cor cried out, and gripped his left side where the poison had struck. Burning pain enveloped his body, and scattered his thoughts, while confused images chased one another through his head.

Cor saw his home and the faces of people he knew. The expression on each face was neither happy nor sad, and it seemed to Cor that they had no names. He saw the rooms and gardens of his father's palace—places where he had grown up—but now they were like words on a piece of paper, one above the other, in a list that had no meaning.

A sour taste, like the acid of shriveled lemons, filled his mouth, and the confusing images sped faster. He couldn't rise from the ground because of the pain in his chest, and he couldn't stop his thoughts that had taken on a life of their own. Endlessly, they drove his exhausted mind, becoming more meaningless the more he tried to understand them.

It seemed like hours, but at last his thoughts began to slow, and the pain became more bearable. Cor found that he was able to sit up. He looked down at his chest, and saw that the wound was gone. His skin was just as it had been before, as if nothing had happened at all. His father had been wrong. The sting of the Dualag hurt, but after all, it wasn't so bad. His chest burned inside, but on the surface nothing could be seen.

Cor laughed. Maybe his father wasn't as smart as he pretended to be. Cor had fought a Dualag, and killed it. Had his father ever done that? Only a warrior who has tasted victory can say he truly knows the enemy, thought Cor. The

rest only pretend. With a satisfied chuckle, he picked up his
sword, and buckled on his armor.

Part 2

The wound from the Dualag didn't heal. It couldn't be seen,
but the pain smoldered beneath Cor's skin. At night restless
dreams disturbed his sleep, and during the day he wore
himself out, arguing back and forth inside his head. Had he
been right to hunt the Necrofang alone after Fletcher's
death? He had killed it, and also a Dualag. He ought to be
proud of what he had done. But a voice inside him
whispered that he had behaved as no fairy knight should,
and the argument began again.

When Cor reached the fortress he told the other fairies
what had happened to Fletcher. No one said anything about
Cor's decision to fight the Necrofang with only Fletcher at
his side. Cor shouldn't have done it, but the other fairies
saw how much he suffered, and they didn't want to add to
his sadness. They tried to comfort him, but there was
something in Cor's eyes that kept them back.

In the days that followed Cor didn't fight as well as he
had before. He slept poorly at night, and was tired during
the day. He was weaker than he had been, and the pain in
his side interfered with his sword work.

"You're injured," said Regador. "Why didn't you tell
me?"

"I didn't want to worry you," said Cor.

Regador made Cor lie down, and examined him. Nothing could be seen, but when he touched the place where the Dualag's tail had scraped across Cor's chest, Cor jerked with pain.

"I've never seen a wound like this," said Regador. "Did you get it fighting the Necrofang?"

"Yes," said Cor.

Regador's eyes narrowed.

"We'll watch it closely," he said, and left Cor alone.

Cor lay still. He didn't know what to think. He hadn't told a lie since he was a small boy.

"That was strange," thought Cor. "Why did I say the wound was from the Necrofang? But what difference does it make? A wound is a wound whether it comes from one beast or another. It would be silly to say anything now. I'd look stupid."

He closed his eyes to try to sleep, and in the darkness he saw his father's face. His mouth was compressed into a tight line.

"Regador!" Cor shouted.

Regador returned.

"Sir, I beg your pardon. I spoke carelessly. It was not the Necrofang that gave me the wound. It was a Dualag."

"A Dualag! How did you meet a Dualag?"

"It was after I killed the Necrofang."

"You're lucky to be alive," said Regador. "But a wound from a Dualag is a serious matter. I've never heard of a fairy surviving a battle with a Dualag, so I don't know much about this kind of wound. But some say..."

He stopped.

"Let me look at it again. Tell me everything that happened. At least we will learn something."

Regador opened Cor's shirt, and gasped. A deep gash ran across Cor's chest. It was black, as if the poison had charred the skin. In some places, the wound was covered with tiny droplets of water, like sweat. In other places it oozed pus. Cor squeezed his eyes shut, and wondered if it would become invisible again.

Cor told Regador what had happened during the battle with the Dualag. He told him how the beast had changed each time he defeated it, and he described the appearance of each of the forms. He told Regador how he had finally cut off the head of the Dualag, and how the tail had struck him after it appeared to be dead.

While Cor spoke, Regador explored the wound with his fingers, felt for heat on Cor's forehead, and pressed the sides of Cor's neck beneath his chin. Finally, he looked into Cor's eyes.

"How do you feel?"

"It burns."

"Anything else?"

"No."

"Have you noticed..." Regador hesitated. There was a period of silence. Finally Regador said, "Tell me if you notice anything. I've heard that the sting of the Dualag can do strange things to a fairy. I think it would be best if you didn't fight until we know the full effects of this injury."

Cor frowned, but said nothing.

He stayed inside the fortress and rested while the other fairy knights continued their battles against the dark beasts. The forced respite seemed to do him good, and it was not long before he felt his strength return. The wound still burned, and the black mark remained, but he felt better, and he persuaded himself that he was fully recovered. He no longer allowed Regador to examine him.

"I'm well, I tell you," said Cor to Regador one day. He laughed. "You'll have to find a new patient to take care of. Let me fight again, and I'll show you just how well I am."

But Regador wouldn't allow him to fight, and Cor grew impatient.

The dark beasts were restless, and they pressed in around the fortress. Cor hated to do nothing while the other fairies fought. Of course, there was work to be done in the fortress; the work of cleaning up, and putting things where they belonged. But it wasn't interesting to Cor, and while his hands moved, his thoughts were someplace else. His work was careless.

He did all he could to persuade Regador to let him fight. He tried to be cheerful, and he pretended the pain from the wound was gone. One day he woke up to find that the black mark had faded from his chest. Everything looked the way it used to. He touched the place where the mark had been, and his face contorted with pain. The wound was still there, it just couldn't be seen. That was good enough for now.

"Look," said Cor, showing his chest to Regador. "Now you can see with your own eyes that I'm well. At the very least let me take my turn on watch tonight. It isn't fair that I get to sleep, while everyone else must do extra duty."

Regador touched the place where the wound had been, and Cor fought to hide the signs of pain from his face. His expression never flickered, but Regador shook his head in silence, and walked away. Later that night, Cor saw Regador and Fyddon sitting in a corner, with their heads close together. They spoke in low voices, and Cor thought he saw them glance in his direction.

There were battles every day, and in the evening, when the fairy knights returned to the fortress, their faces were flushed with victory. At night they gathered around the fire, and told stories of the day's battles. Cor sat at the edge of the group, a smile frozen on his face, covering the resentment that burned in his throat.

* * *

All except the watch were asleep when Cor left the fortress of the fairy knights. No one saw him go, and he left no note. He traveled for days without purpose. He had no desire now to hunt the dark beasts.

One day he came upon a village. He saw a fairy maiden picking mushrooms that grew among the roots of the trees. She heard him approach, and stood up.

"You are a fairy knight," she said, looking at his armor. "Why have you come here? There are no beasts to hunt in this part of the forest."

She was slender, and her eyes were calm like the summer sea. She said her name was Naida. Cor could see that she had never known fear.

"This place lies within the Dark Forest," said Cor. "How is it that the beasts don't come here?"

Naida knelt down, and resumed picking mushrooms. She placed the mushrooms one-by-one in her basket as she spoke.

"Many years ago, this village was visited by a fairy no one had ever seen before. He asked for something to eat, and when he had finished his meal, he played on a harp made of silver. Those who were there said the harp never made a sound, but every time his fingers plucked a note, threads of light flew in every direction. They twisted through the air, and disappeared. His music wove a net around us that no evil has ever been able to penetrate.

Cor wondered if this was a place where he could find a cure for the Dualag's sting.

"I would like to stay here, if I may" he said. "I've fought for too long, and I need rest."

"I can take you to my father," said Naida. "But where are your friends? I've heard that the fairy knights never travel alone."

Cor frowned, and studied Naida's face. What did she suspect? But he looked into her eyes, and his suspicions disappeared. Once again he thought that here was a place where he might be healed. Cor decided he would tell Naida about the Dualag's wound, but not yet. She might be like the others, and not understand. So he said,

"I travel alone to prove my worth as a knight. I fought a Necrofang, and I defeated it. And there is another beast that

I killed as well, more powerful even than the Necrofang. You are right that the fairy knights have always fought together, but destiny has set me apart from all others."

Naida said nothing, and Cor followed her back to the village.

Naida's mother and father welcomed Cor, and invited him to stay with them. The village fairies wanted Cor to tell them stories of his adventures, but Cor spoke little. In the evening, he sat silently by the fire, staring into the flames, sometimes looking up at Naida, who sat near her mother some distance away from him.

Despite his plan to find a cure for the Dualag's wound, Cor said nothing about it. He spent most days walking with Naida. His wound hurt less when he was with her. But as they walked, Naida kept her eyes on the ground, reaching down occasionally to put a mushroom in her basket.

Over time, Naida became more distant. Cor saw that she avoided him, and his face flushed when he thought of it. What was wrong with her? Didn't she know who he was? Everyone else admired him, because he had done what no fairy knight had ever done before.

Cor wished she could see him in battle. He imagined himself rescuing her village from attack. But there were no dark beasts here, and he cursed the enchantment that kept them away.

One day, a villager who had gone out to fetch water early in the morning brought back news of a white stag he had seen drinking from the stream. He said the antlers of the stag had flashed in the light of the sun, and it was thought to be the Silver Stag, the legendary animal that grants wishes to those swift enough to catch it. Everyone hoped to see this magical creature. When Cor heard the news, he swore an oath that he would capture it, and give the wish to Naida.

Cor knew he might have only a single chance, so he stayed up all night making preparations. In the darkness he roamed the forest, setting traps. By sunrise all was complete, and he crouched among the reeds by the side of the stream where hoof prints of the Silver Stag made triangles in the mud.

In the gathering light of dawn, the stag emerged from the forest, its antlers gleaming in the morning sun. It walked to the edge of the water, bent its neck, and drank.

In a moment Cor was out of the reeds and on the stag's back. He threw a halter of rope over its head, but the rope caught on the silver antlers, and was cut to pieces. The powerful animal threw Cor into the air, then shook its head and charged up the forest path. Cor followed, half a dozen paces behind.

Ahead of them was a net that Cor had strung between two trees on either side of the path. It was hidden by leaves he had woven among the cords. The stag ran directly toward it.

"I have you now," thought Cor.

But the silver antlers swept the net aside as if it were nothing but a spider web, and the stag's pounding legs carried it forward along the forest path.

The path began to curve in a wide arc, and Cor took a sharp turn through the underbrush. He knew a shortcut that would allow him to get in front of the stag. Thorns ripped his clothes and scratched his skin, but Cor didn't slow his pace. Soon the shortcut brought him back to the path, just ahead of the running stag.

It came charging around the bend, almost crashing into Cor, its legs a confused tangle as it tried to stop. Clumps of dirt flew into the air, covering the stag with dust. It backed against a wall of rock that ran alongside the path, and Cor drew his sword.

"You are mine, beast," he said, advancing on the Silver Stag. "Do not make me slay you. I claim your wish."

The stag bent its hind legs, and sprang into the air. Cor watched its pale belly pass over his head, and ducked to avoid the sharp hooves. He returned his sword to its sheath, and ran after the fleeing animal.

The path now led close to the village, and the two runners passed by groups of fairies who had come out to watch. Out of the corner of his eye Cor saw Naida, and he increased his speed. The stag's coat was covered with sweat; it's pace was slower than before, then it stumbled.

Hidden under a layer of leaves, the path was covered with logs that rolled beneath the weight of the stag. Each time it tried to regain its footing, it stepped on another log. It stumbled again and again, until finally it fell. Cor leaped upon the stag, and pinned it to the ground.

Cor's shirt had been torn when he took the shortcut through the thorny brush, and as he wrestled with the stag, his bare chest touched the soft hair that covered the animal's side. The invisible wound of the Dualag pressed against the stag, and it shrieked.

Cor had never heard a sound like that. It was a scream of pain and fear, and Cor jumped with surprise. The stag threw him off, and got back on its feet. There was foam at the edges of the its mouth, and its eyes were shot with red. Its thin legs scrambled in the dirt as it struggled to get away.

Cor's nostrils flared. The ugly scream still rang in his ears. He drew a knife from a leather sheath strapped to his ankle, and threw. The blade hissed through the air, struck the stag's flank, and cut deep. Cor charged the wounded animal, crashed into it with his shoulder, and brought it down for the last time.

The stag lay on the ground, breathing heavily, its coat covered in blood. Cor looked up, and saw Naida standing over them, her round eyes fixed on the wounded animal. Cor gripped the base of the stag's antlers, and pressed its head hard into the dirt. He looked up at Naida with glowing eyes.

"I have captured the beast," he said. "The wish is yours."

The stag moved its head in the dust in a useless attempt to escape the grip of the fairy. Naida's lips trembled. She tried to speak, but the words caught in her throat. Finally she took a ragged breath.

"Go away," she said. "Go away, and never come back."

She covered her face with her hands as she stifled a sob, then ran back to the village.

Cor watched until he could see her no longer, then looked down at the stag. It's black eyes were like a mirror that reflected the wound on his chest. The reflection showed a wound that was dark, swollen, and now covered his entire left side.

Blood flowed down the stag's side, pooling on the ground. It had stopped struggling. Cor bowed his head.

"I wish it were as if we had never met," he said in a low voice, and he was alone. On his chest was the mark of the Dualag's sting, visible once more, just as he had seen it in the Silver Stag's eyes.

The stag stood some distance away. Its coat gleamed pure white. It turned its back on Cor, and disappeared among the trees.

* * *

The springtime was damp. Cold drizzle fell from the sky, and Cor was wet most of the time. He walked through the woods with a pace that changed little, whether the sun was shining, or rain soaked the ground. Sometimes he slept during the day and sometimes at night.

The warm weather brought flowers that grew near the forest path, but Cor didn't notice. Green leaves appeared on the trees, which now stood farther apart from one another, opening up the woods, and making it easier to walk.

Night came, and the moon rose above the trees. Cor heard the hooting of an owl among the branches of a tree, and the rustling of tiny feet over the pine needles that covered the ground. The wound on his chest burned, and Cor wondered if he could ever go home.

Ahead of him he saw the Silver Stag, standing perfectly

still in the moonlight. As Cor drew near, the stag began to walk, and Cor followed. The stag led him through a grove of birch trees. The edges of their papery bark were sharpened like razors by the moonlight. They walked until they reached a clearing where the birch trees grew in a circle, and in the center was a pool of water.

Cor walked to the edge of the pool, and looked down. The reflection of his face was cruel and misshapen. He stared into the pool for a long time. When he looked up, the stag was gone.

He was thirsty after his long walk, so he reached into the water with cupped hands, and drank. The water tasted salty. His throat burned, and a spasm of pain tore through his body. Cor choked, and scrambled away from the bank.

"It's poisoned," he thought, gasping for breath. "The stag has taken its revenge."

But soon the pain subsided, and Cor approached the pool again, unable to tear his eyes away from the darkness that obscured his face. He thought of Naida, who ran from him. He thought of the fairy knights, who wouldn't let him fight, and of Regador, who distrusted him.

"None of them understands," he thought. "The Dualag wounded me, but I killed it. No fairy has ever done that before."

He sat by the side of the pool, thinking. By his own strength he had lifted himself beyond the rank of any fairy knight. The mark on his chest burned—its darkness made his face terrible. But it was the mark of his victory over the greatest beast in the forest, perhaps in all the world.

"They pretend that what I did counts for nothing," thought Cor. "Three times I fought the Dualag, and three times I saw it fall."

He was the first among the fairy knights. It was the greatness he had wished for all along. But the high place was a lonely one. Cor thought of the other knights, and the many battles they had fought together. They hated him now. They envied him. That was why they tried to deny the greatness of all he had accomplished. But maybe he had the power to force them to see the truth.

No one understood the beasts as he did. The reflection in the pool showed that the Dualag's sting was bringing him closer to those who ruled this forest. As the wound grew larger, and the shadow sank deeper, he approached nearer to the source of their power.

The dark beasts were strong, he thought, but the fairies overcame them in battle. The beasts couldn't stand against the well-planned attacks of the fairy knights working together. But Cor could change that. Royal blood flowed through his veins, and with the power that came from the Dualag's sting, he could make the beasts obey him. He didn't have to resist the poison of the Dualag, he thought, he could use it. It would no longer be a curse, but a charm of mighty strength.

Cor narrowed his eyes in concentration until they were two thin slits.

The truth of the sting depended on how you looked at it. There was no right way or wrong way. You could fight against it and die, or embrace it and grow strong. Why not grasp the power that burned within him? The Dualag's sting would be his final connection to the beasts. He would be their master, and they would be his servants. Together they would conquer.

Cor stood up. His face was hard. No one would ever question his valor again. He looked down into the pool one last time, and within its depths he saw a face that was not his own. He looked again, and saw that it was the face of his father. The expression was sad and stern and kind all at once. The lips didn't move, but Cor heard the words,

"I understand how it is. No matter how you choose, you are my son."

Then the image was gone, and Cor was alone again. He took a step toward the trees, then stopped. At last he turned back, knelt by the pool, and drank. With the first mouthful he felt his strength drain away. After the second his throat convulsed with violent choking, and he felt that he couldn't drink a single drop more. But he did. He drank until he thought it would kill him, and then he lay down by the side of the pool to die.

He lay there for a long time. All the doubts were gone now. He was going to die, and he didn't need to fight, or even think, anymore. After a while he fell asleep, and dreamed of his home. Above him stood his mother and father. He looked up into their faces, and they smiled.

Cor opened his eyes, and stood up. He felt unsteady, but inside him a new strength was born; a strength of patience, of watching, and waiting. On his chest a red scar marked the place where the Dualag's wound had been. He leaned over the water, and the pool reflected his old, familiar face. It was thinner than before, but the shadow was gone, and his eyes were clear, like the eyes of the Silver Stag.

A fresh wind blew, and white clouds skidded across the sky. Cor looked around as if seeing the world for the first time. Ahead of him were the foothills of the Eastern Mountains, and behind him was the vast expanse of the forest. The birch trees waived their branches in the wind, and Cor began to walk; back to the fortress of the fairy knights, who battled the beasts that haunted the woods, and were said to be fearless.

THE FAIRY WHO BECAME MORTAL

In a quiet valley, far from the cities and towns where humans live, grew an old forest. Here the trees stretched up to the sky, and even on the hottest days it was cool and shady beneath their branches. The ground was thick with ferns and fallen leaves, and green moss crept up the gnarled roots that buried themselves in the dirt. Robins, bluebirds, and sparrows flew among the branches, and filled the air with their songs.

This was a place where fairies lived. There was a whole kingdom of fairies here. There was a fairy king, a fairy queen, fairy nobles, fairy knights, and even ordinary fairies, if "ordinary" is a word that can be used to describe a fairy.

In a warm and sunny part of the forest there lived a fairy whose name was Flora. Her job was to take care of the flowers that grew there. Although she wasn't very big, she was very beautiful. In fact, she believed she was the most beautiful fairy in the entire forest. Flora was young by fairy standards, but as far as anyone knows, fairies live forever, so their standards are different from our own.

Flora's job was to visit the flowers every day, and work her enchantments early in the morning when they were wet with dew. Flowers love to drink the morning dew, especially when it's been enchanted by a fairy, and each morning they eagerly awaited Flora's arrival.

There were times, however, when the thirsty flowers were disappointed. Anyone who saw Flora would think she was the perfect model of what a fairy ought to be, but Flora loved to go to parties. She stayed up late, and when morning came, she slept in.

Whenever she went out, Flora was surrounded by admirers, who competed with one another for her attention. They played at falling in love, and Flora danced with the ones who sighed the deepest, or looked at her with the most longing eyes. Fairies learn about love from the stories that are told about humans, and they think it's the funniest, silliest, most delightful game in the world.

One day the eldest son of the King of the Fairies came to dance at one of the fairy balls. He had heard about Flora's beauty, and wanted to see her with his own eyes. He came from a part of the forest where dangerous beasts lurked. The prince was a valiant fairy knight who defended the kingdom, and made sure no harm came to his father's subjects. His name was Cor. He traveled in the simple clothes of a soldier. At his belt hung a sword that was decorated with a small diamond set into the hilt. It represented the royal insignia—a single star, shining in the night sky.

The prince was a seasoned warrior who had learned to face the enemy with a clear head and a steady hand, but when he saw Flora for the first time, his thoughts scattered, and all he could do was stare. After a moment, he recovered himself, and walked over to where she sat. He bowed, and asked her to dance. Flora held out her pretty hand, and Cor led her onto the dance floor, which was overhung with white flowers, and illuminated with the glow of fireflies.

Flora was charmed with the prince, and danced with him many times that night. Not only was he the eldest son of the King of the Fairies, but she thought he played at being in love better than anyone else.

The prince, however, was not so charmed with Flora. He was overcome by her beauty, but he also saw that she was a terrible flirt. When she danced with him, she sent secret glances to her other admirers. If Cor sat down with her on some secluded bench, she called the others to join them, then jumped up, and skipped away, laughing. Cor was left alone with deep lines creasing his forehead.

Days went by, and Cor tried to make excuses for Flora. He tried to persuade himself there were reasons for all the things she did. But he couldn't deceive himself forever, and one day he said,

"She is beautiful, but she is not good. Tomorrow I will leave this place, and return to the Dark Forest. I'll do battle with the most ferocious beasts I can find, and soon I'll forget her."

But when the next day arrived, the prince did not leave. Night after night he swore that he would go away, but each morning he found some new reason to stay, and the lines on his forehead grew deeper.

Prince Cor had fallen in love with Flora, which was an unusual thing. True love is almost unheard of among the fairies. It's thought that only humans really fall in love. It may have been that Prince Cor was different from other fairies because of his time in the Dark Forest. Something had happened to him there, and he had become capable of experiencing the kinds of feelings humans have.

Fairies don't think much of humans. Compared to fairies, humans are clumsy, stupid creatures, who are easily tricked. They're much too big, and worst of all, they're mortal. After a while, they die. They're not like the fairies, who as far as anyone knows, live forever.

Prince Cor decided he would try to make Flora more worthy of his love. In the evening he sat with her on a grassy hill while they watched the sun set, and he spoke to her about serious things. At first, Flora didn't enjoy these talks, but she put up with them. It was funny to see the expressions on the other fairies' faces when she carelessly mentioned that the prince had invited her to spend the evening with him again. Flora told them with a laugh that he was wearing her out with his attentions.

Over time, however, she began to enjoy their talks more. The prince looked handsome in the light of the setting sun, and the expression on his face was earnest. And yet, it was hard for her to understand the things he said. So she did something that was unusual for her. She tried. She didn't do it because he was the eldest son of the King of the Fairies, she did it because it seemed important to him. Many fairies had played at falling in love with her, but none of them had really cared much about it. Flora decided she liked Prince Cor the best.

So Flora tried, but she wasn't good at it. Trying made her tired, and she gave up. She begged the prince to take her to parties again, where she danced and flirted, and forgot all the things he had told her. In the end, the prince left. How could someone so beautiful be so heartless, he wondered. He did not return to the royal palace, or to the dark places of the forest. He disappeared without a trace, and no one could tell what had become of him.

* * *

Flora missed the prince after he was gone. The games of love the other fairies played had become tiresome. She tried to teach them how to look at her the way Prince Cor had done, but none of them could manage it. She wanted to teach them how to speak to her about serious things, but she couldn't remember what the serious things were. In the evening she sat on the grassy hill, watching the red clouds deepen to black, trying to remember what Cor had told her. She had stopped going to parties, so she had lots of time to sit on the hill and think.

Now that she wasn't staying out late anymore, Flora

could pay more attention to her flowers. They said the dews she prepared had acquired a new flavor, and were more filling. Some even thought their stems grew stronger. Flora became more interested in the flowers she cared for, and in return they told her their secrets.

The flowers spoke to her in whispers when the stars came out at night, and in the morning they taught Flora the songs that all flowers learn on the first day when they open their petals to greet the rising sun. The secrets of the flowers reminded Flora of the things the prince used to say, but they were easier for her to understand. She made the flowers tell her everything they knew.

Soon the trees, too, wanted to share their secrets with the beautiful fairy, and they invited her to come and sit among their branches. Flora went at night, when the fireflies made the underside of the leaves glow orange. There, in a world of glimmering light, the trees spoke to her of the old truths they had learned hundreds of years ago; truths that were older than the forest itself. The secrets of the trees were very much like the things the prince had spoken of, and at last Flora began to understand.

"I must find the prince," she thought. "He will be proud of me."

Flora knew that Prince Cor had disappeared, but she thought she could find him. She knew that he had loved her, but she didn't know if he loved her still. She was determined to find out.

She said goodbye to her flowers, and set off into the woods. She searched for months, but no one could tell her what had happened to the prince. The younger fairies thought she wanted to play a game, and offered to fall in love with her themselves. Flora became angry with them, and sent them away. The oldest and wisest fairies only looked at her gravely, and shook their heads in silence. That was even more provoking, and Flora stamped her foot in frustration.

Then one day, Flora found a clue. A bluebell told Flora that she might have seen the prince.

"He was sick," said the flower. "He asked if he could lie down next to me and die. It frightened me, so I made him go away."

"Where did he go?"

"There's an old fairy who lives at the top of the hill who comes to ask the flowers for their nectar. I thought she might be able to help him. He said he didn't think anyone could, but he would fight to the end. His words made me sad."

But Flora was already gone. She was racing toward the top of the hill.

The cottage on the hill was painted white. It had open shutters on all the windows, and was covered with honeysuckle. The air around the cottage smelled sweet, but Flora didn't notice. She ran to the door, knocked quickly, and entered almost before she heard the words, "Come in."

"Where is he? Is he alive?"

"He's not here, but I think he is alive" said an old fairy who sat in a rocking chair next to one of the open windows. "Who are you?"

Flora told the old fairy who she was, and why she was looking for Prince Cor.

"Please tell me where he is," said Flora. "I need to find him."

"He's gone away."

"Where did he go?"

"That's not important. I did all I could for him, but I'm afraid that now he can't come back."

"But where did he go?"

"Sit down, Flora, and I will give you something to drink. It will make you feel better."

The old fairy stood up, took a cup from a shelf, and filled it with drops of bright liquid, first from one bottle, then another. Some of the drops were red, some purple, and some golden. As they fell, the drops sparkled like tiny jewels. In a little while, steam came out of the cup, and the cottage was filled with the smell of baking apples. Flora felt more calm, and she looked around the room. It was a comfortable room with cushioned chairs. Pots and pans hung from the ceiling, and crackling sticks burned in a large stone fireplace .

"Where is he?" she asked again in a quiet voice.

The old fairy handed the cup to Flora, who put it down on the table in front of her. They looked at one another for a while. Then the old fairy said,

"There was something wrong with him. Do you know what it was?"

Flora looked down at the table, but didn't speak.

"He had a broken heart. That's a strange thing for a fairy

to have."

Still Flora said nothing.

"Fairies can't survive a broken heart. It kills them," said the old fairy.

"You said he was alive!"

"He is. Fairies cannot survive a broken heart, but there are others who can."

"Who?"

"Humans."

Flora gasped.

"Humans die—they're mortal."

The old fairy frowned. "Do you really know what it means to be human?"

"No."

"Nobody does."

Flora looked at the cup in front of her. Its soothing fragrance still hung in the air, but Flora's heart beat fast.

"Did he want to become human?"

"He knew nothing about it. By the time he reached me, it was almost too late. I had to act quickly in order to save him. The potion to change him was made in a hurry, and badly, I'm afraid. It's a difficult potion, and the preparation should be slow. Many things may have gone wrong, but I believe he survived.

"Flora, do you blame me for what I did? Was I wrong to save his life? Fairies don't understand as much about humans as we think we do. They can be foolish creatures, but there are things humans know that fairies do not. There are things humans can become that fairies cannot."

"Will Cor know those things?"

"Yes."

"And become those things?"

"No one knows what a human will become. They choose for themselves."

Flora was silent for a time, then she took a deep breath.

"I will know those things, and do those things. I will follow Cor, and become human, too."

"No," said the old fairy. "I made Cor human because he was dying. Drink your tea, Flora. You'll feel better. Soon you'll go back to your flowers, and you will forget him."

Flora looked down at the cup. The old fairy muttered some words, and thick steam rose from the surface of the liquid. The moist heat warmed Flora's face, and made her sleepy. Confused thoughts filled her head, and everything around her seemed unreal. She became unsure of where she was.

"Back with my flowers I will forget him," she said, as if speaking to herself. The sleepy feeling grew stronger. "I will be a flower fairy, and I will never die. Every day I will see the sun rise, and every day I will see it set. Every spring I will see the flowers bloom, and every fall I will see them die. A fairy's life is like a circle."

"Yes, a fairy's life is a circle. A perfect circle."

"Is a human's life like a circle?"

"No. For a human every day is different. Humans get somewhere."

Flora thought about what that would be like. In her mind she saw streams of days stretching far into the future, no two of them the same; days like enchanted doors opening into the unknown.

Flora thought of Cor, who would wake each morning, not knowing who he would become until the moment he had to choose. Cor was human now, and he couldn't stand still. For better or for worse, Cor would get somewhere, and in the end, he would leave her far behind.

She shook herself awake. She would not return to her flowers. She would not go back to the parties, to the balls, and to the fairies who pretended to love.

"I have gotten somewhere," she said. "I will become human, and find Prince Cor."

"No," said the old fairy. "You will not."

Flora stood up. She picked up the cup with the sweet-smelling liquid, and poured it into the fire. There was a look on her face that the old fairy had never seen before. It rather shocked her.

Flora remained in the neighborhood of the old fairy, and every day she came to the cottage, and asked to be turned into a human. Flora's voice was quiet, but she made it clear that she would never stop. It didn't take long for the old fairy to give in.

"If you choose to be human," she said, "you can never come back."

"I will follow the prince," said Flora.

"Then I will send you to the human city of Anthrones. It is the royal city, where the king has built his palace. The prince is there, but I warn you, you will find him much changed. He is so changed, that I wonder if you will even recognize him. The world of humans is not like ours, Flora. You will need to keep your eyes open."

Days went by as Flora watched the old fairy prepare the potion that would make Flora human. Pots bubbled and kettles hissed, as one by one the ingredients were made ready. The old fairy worked slowly. She wanted to make sure that no harm would come to Flora when the transformation occurred.

At last it was ready. The old fairy poured the dark liquid into a cup, and handed it to Flora. Flora held the cup in both hands. It was warm. Outside the open window she heard the humming of bees as they gathered nectar from the honeysuckle. A breeze made the pots and pans hanging from the ceiling sway back and forth. Flora took one last look around the room, breathed in, and drank.

She breathed out, and found herself alone, walking down an unfamiliar road.

* * *

Flora felt sick. Her head was heavy, and everything about her was too big. Her foot scraped against the road, and she stumbled. Flora looked down at her oversized arms and legs, and wondered if she was still beautiful. She was, but now she was a beautiful woman, rather than a beautiful fairy.

After walking for half an hour, Flora reached the edge of the town. Anthrones was built on a hill by the side of the sea. There was a harbor where ships of all nations docked.

Close by there were shops that sold compasses, lumber, and nails. Rows of houses formed ever smaller circles as they neared the summit.

The water sparkled in the sun, dazzling Flora's eyes. Up and down the hill she saw people sitting out on balconies, enjoying the fine weather. Gulls circled the harbor, screeching to one another. Flora looked around, confused by the unfamiliar sights and sounds, and she wondered how she would ever find the prince in this great city. Her eyes followed the main road up the hill. Higher and higher it climbed until it reached the very top where the king's palace lay. Green lawns dotted with trees formed a park that surrounded the palace. Spires rose into the sky, and a golden dome flashed in the sun.

Flora remembered the words of the old fairy: *You must keep your eyes open.* She gazed on the beauty of the palace.

"That's where I will find him," she thought, and continued along the road that led to the top of the hill.

When Flora arrived at the palace, she met a girl playing in the gardens who gazed at her in wonder. Flora looked down, and smiled.

"I like the way she smiles," thought the girl. "I have never seen anyone so beautiful. I wonder if she's a princess." Then she said out loud, "Who are you, and where have you come from?"

"My name is Flora, and I have come from far away. I've come to see the prince."

The girl ran to tell the others that the most beautiful woman in the world had come to the palace from a distant land, and that she must be a princess. A delegation was quickly put together to welcome her. The queen thought it was unusual that a princess would arrive all alone with no attendants or even baggage, but she attributed it to the strange ways of foreigners.

"These days, the behavior of all young princesses is quite impossible," the queen explained to the king. "Who can say what foreign princesses won't do?"

So Flora was given a room in the castle, and the queen provided her with everything she needed.

The prince had been away for a long time, and word had reached the king and queen that he was on his way home. He was returning from a journey he had undertaken in search of a wife. The king felt it was time for him to marry, but none of the ladies at the court had been able to win his heart. Some said that the prince would not marry because he was too fond of hunting, good wine, and late nights. But the prince was a noble-looking man, and these complaints were dismissed as nothing but spite.

The prince had traveled among the neighboring kingdoms, and then to lands that lay over the seas. Many rumors had reached the palace regarding his travels. Some said he had sailed over the edge of the world, others said he had plunged to the bottom of the sea, and fallen in love with a mermaid. The most hopeful news told of a princess who lived in the land of Norvalia. It was said that the prince had declared his love for her, and that a wedding was planned. But in the end, nothing had come of it, and the prince was returning alone.

When he arrived at the palace, he greeted his mother and father.

"We are glad you have come home safe," said the queen. "But we had hoped you would bring with you one whom we could welcome as a daughter."

"My journey did not prosper in the way I had hoped," said the prince.

"We heard you had found someone who pleased you in the kingdom of Norvalia. Was it not true? It was said that everything was settled."

"I'm afraid it was not true, Mother. The king of Norvalia has a pretty daughter who possesses a great wit. It pleased us both to walk in each other's company, and dance together at the balls. And so the story reached you, embellished by it's journey of a thousand miles."

"And what was wrong with her, my son?" asked the queen.

"There was nothing wrong with her, Mother. But I could not love her."

"It is not well to set one's standards so high that none can meet them," said the king.

"Is it wrong to take care in choosing the one who will someday wear the crown that sits on my mother's head?" asked the prince.

"It is not. Such care is fitting. It is not fitting, however, to delay for reasons that reflect poorly upon the duties of a prince."

"Father, you wrong me."

"Do I? Then find her. Find the one who is right."

A ball was held that night to celebrate the prince's return. Flora wondered what he would look like. She wondered if he would remember her, or if his sudden change into a human had affected his memory.

The ladies of the court were also anxious for the arrival of the prince. He remained unmarried, so it was still possible that he could fall in love at any moment. Besides, he was a graceful dancer, and had the most charming manners. Everyone agreed that no ball was complete without him.

The prince arrived late, and his entrance caused a stir. At first it was hard for Flora to see him, because he was surrounded by so many young ladies. But eventually the crowd thinned, and she saw that he was indeed handsome, but handsome in a way that was different from how she remembered him. His hair was long and carefully curled, and he was dressed in magnificent clothes.

He smiled at everyone. He seemed happier now than he had been when he was a fairy. Flora remembered him as being serious, with deep lines in his forehead.

"Although I suppose those lines were because of me," she thought. "I wonder if he is happier now because he has forgotten me."

The prince made his way around the room, greeting the guests. When he reached Flora, he stared at her beauty, and wondered that he had never seen her at a ball before. She curtsied to the prince.

"Good evening, Your Highness," she said. "I am so happy to see you. I wonder if you remember me."

The prince's memory was poor, so he said, "Of course, I do. But tonight you are looking more beautiful than I have ever seen you look before."

Flora blushed. "He still loves me, even though I'm no longer a flower fairy," she thought.

Flora danced with the prince many times that night, but her joy at having found him was tempered by concern. She thought of the sickness he had suffered during his last days as a fairy, and the dangerous effects of drinking the potion that had been made in haste. His memory of her was vague, and he avoided the subject of the past. When she mentioned their previous lives as fairies, he laughed, and thought she was making a joke. Sometimes he was distracted by other young ladies who danced close to him, and smiled.

But Flora remembered the fairy prince she loved, and she said to herself,

"When I first met him, I thought of nothing but parties and admirers. He helped me find my true self, and I will do the same for him."

Flora believed that if she could make him remember his life as a fairy, he would once again become the Prince Cor he used to be.

As the days went by, the prince spent a great deal of time with Flora. Sometimes he found it hard to understand the things she said, but he was captivated by her beauty. She was different from the other ladies of the court, who flattered him with empty complements. She didn't seem to care about his rank, and yet, he knew that in her quiet way she cared more about him than anyone else. He suspected that she had fallen in love with him.

"The lady who arrived at the palace a short while ago seems to have found favor in your eyes," said the king to his son one evening, as they sat down to dinner.

"Yes, Father. She is very beautiful."

"And you enjoy her company?"

"I would rather be with her than with anyone else, excepting Your Majesty and my mother."

"I'm glad to hear it. Now tell me, what more do you want? Let this be a time of joy for all the kingdom. If you will marry her, I will give you the summer palace as a wedding gift. I will fill the stables with horses, the kennels with dogs, and the cellars with good wine. You shall choose everything. Come, what do you say?"

"Father, there is no need to persuade me to do the thing that my heart has already decided upon."

"It is well chosen. I stand by my promise, however. The summer palace shall be yours."

"You have always been the most generous of fathers," said the prince.

That evening the prince walked with Flora in the rose garden, where the air was heavy with the scent of flowers. He turned to her, and took both her hands in his.

"You have been here only a short time," he said, "but I feel as if I have known you all my life."

"I searched for you for such a long time."

"I have searched for a long time, also. There have been many who have thought to lead me to this garden, Flora, but none was like you."

"After you left, I tried to make myself worthy of you."

"You did well to prepare yourself. It is a great responsibility to be queen. All eyes will be upon you, and how you act in public will be a matter of great importance. But Flora, I, myself, am easy to please. A man likes to have his simple pleasures, and I am no different from any other. But as my wife, you will have all you need to make you happy. My father gives us the summer palace for a wedding present, and your beauty will grace the most magnificent balls anyone has ever seen. I promise you that the countryside will speak of nothing else."

"Do not tease me, Prince. I am not the same as I was before."

"Don't worry, Flora. You'll be fine. Just do as I tell you, remember your position, and none will deny that she whom I have chosen is the finest lady in the kingdom."

Flora promised to do everything the prince asked.

* * *

The prince's engagement to Flora was a pleasant time for him. The wedding date was set, and each day he felt himself drawn closer to her gentle nature. He allowed himself to speak openly to her about his hopes and burdens.

Flora felt his growing trust, but she worried that she got no closer to waking the fairy prince within him. He was different than he had been before. At times she was startled by some of the things he said, and in her darkest moments she feared that the Prince Cor she had loved was gone forever.

A few miles from the palace grew a forest. Although there were no fairies in this forest, it felt like a friendly place. The trees and flowers didn't speak to Flora, but she thought they knew who she was. Today, she needed their comfort. The prince was becoming more and more unlike his true self, and she didn't know what to do. Flora walked among the trees, hoping the woods would provide her with an answer.

She knelt down beside a patch of primroses, and whispered, "Which of your songs did the prince love best?"

But the primroses were silent.

An ancient tree grew nearby, its thick branches stretching high above her head.

"What must I do to help the prince remember?"

The wind blew through the leaves of the tree, but no other answer was given.

All of a sudden, Flora felt she could stand it no longer.

"Don't you remember me?" she cried out. "I am all alone in this world. Don't you know that I need your help?"

The forest was silent. Flora turned, and walked back toward the palace.

Flora had wandered deep into the woods, and when she emerged into the open air, she found she had lost her way among the twisting paths. She had come out on the far side of the forest, instead of the side nearest to the town. She would have to take a different way back, one that was longer, and now it was late in the day. The sun was setting, and the clouds on the western horizon were dark, like black mountains towering above the earth. Flora hurried down the road.

The wind made Flora's hair fly in all directions. Trees waved their branches, whispering *Shhhhh* to the meadows and fields. Flora quickened her pace. For a long time she walked alone, the only traveler out at this time of night. Then she saw ahead of her a young man sitting by the side of the road. His arms were wrapped around his knees, and his eyes were fixed on the ground. No one was with him. Flora crossed to the opposite side of the road, as she passed.

A few minutes later, she heard footsteps. She looked back, and saw the young man coming toward her.

"Excuse me," he said. "I'm sorry to bother you, but I wonder if you could tell me whether we have we met?"

"No," said Flora. "I have never seen you before. I don't know anybody in this part of the world."

The young man sighed. His gaze fell to the ground. "Thank you," was all he said.

Flora asked the young man his name.

"I wish I could tell you," he said. "Some time ago I became ill, and although I regained my health, something happened to me while I was sick, and I have never been the same since. I cannot remember anything of my prior life, and I don't even know my own name. I travel the kingdom in the hope that someday I will find someone who recognizes me, and then I will know who I am."

Flora looked at him again. His face was gentle, and it

would have been handsome were it not so dirty. She felt sorry for him, but her mind was occupied with thoughts of the prince, and it was hard to think about anything else.

Night had fallen, and the young man offered to walk with her. When they reached the palace gates, Flora said goodbye. The young man looked so sad, that she wanted to say something to comfort him. But it's hard to offer comfort when one's own life is in turmoil. Flora looked around, trying to find something to say.

"The world is a stranger place than I ever imagined," was all she could think of.

It was an odd thing to say, and perhaps not very comforting. But the young man understood what she meant, and he was grateful.

Flora passed through the palace gates, and the young man stood watching her. At last he turned, and disappeared into the night.

* * *

The day of the wedding approached, and Flora redoubled her efforts to help the prince. They spoke together often, but still he found it hard to understand her. At best, she was confusing, and sometimes she made no sense at all. So the prince watched her beautiful face as she talked, and thought about other things.

"I am not able to interest you today," said Flora. "Tell me what you're thinking, and I will try to be more amusing."

The prince had been hoping for a chance to tell Flora about his troubles. He leaned forward, and spoke in a low voice.

"As you know, a ball will be held tonight for my younger brother. It's his birthday, and he will be the guest of honor. I, of course, will be nobody. But I have commissioned the royal goldsmith to design a pendant that I think will not go unnoticed."

The prince smiled as he imagined the scene. Then he became serious again.

"But, Flora, I am plagued with worry. The pendant must be exactly right. I know the goldsmith well, and I have reason to mistrust his judgment. You won't think me rude if I leave you, will you? I'll feel better if I know how things are progressing. I will see you this evening, my love. If all goes well, tonight will be a noble entertainment indeed!"

The prince laughed.

"Watch for the expression on my brother's face," he said. "You will see!"

And he hurried out the door.

The pendant met every expectation of the prince, and caused a great sensation at the ball. As a result, he spent little time with Flora. If the pendant had been a failure, he would have found comfort being by her side. Tonight, however, he was too busy moving around the room, telling everyone how much he hated jewelry, and explaining that he only wore the pendant out of respect for the occasion of his brother's birthday. It was a great shame, he said, that his brother was in a bad temper, and didn't seem to be enjoying the celebration.

Flora stood at the edge of the ballroom. The air was hot, and she felt she was suffocating. Nearby was the entrance to a tower that overlooked the gardens. Flora hurried through the door, and climbed the stairs. When she reached the top, a fresh breeze rustled her gown, and she breathed the cool evening air. In the east a single star had come out, shining bright in the darkening sky.

She knew now that the fairy prince she had loved was gone. The spark of his former self had gone out, and the man who remained—the man she had promised to marry— made her shudder. She wanted to flee. It didn't matter that everyone would blame her. The ladies of the court thought her the most fortunate person in the world. No one would understand what she did. Then Flora thought of the young man who traveled the world in search of the one who knew his name, and she thought that he would understand.

She looked out over the countryside, still visible in the fading light. The tower was high, and Flora could see in every direction. She felt a momentary sense of freedom, but then she thought of the wedding that came closer every day.

How long would she be with this man? She was mortal now, so it couldn't go on forever. One day her life would end, and then everything would be over. Whether she married the prince, or whether she ran away, wouldn't change that. Was that what it meant to be mortal? That her life didn't matter, because someday it would end in nothing.

She could never love the prince, but she had promised to marry him, and she felt she should be true to her promise.

But did promises matter now? When her life was over, everything would be over—including promises kept or broken. It didn't matter whether she was true or false to the man she did not love. Everyone died, and nothing mattered.

Then Flora remembered the songs of her flowers and the secrets of the trees. In her mind she saw the patient eyes of the fairy prince who wanted her to know the beauty that lay at the heart of the world. She might be mortal, she thought, but some things were not. Some things had no beginning and would have no end.

Flora thought of the evenings when she sat with Cor on the hill. She could see his face as he tried to make her understand. The man she had promised to marry was the ghost of the man she loved. But here at last, at the top of the tower where the air blew clear upon her face, she had finally found something that reminded her of Cor.

How terrible it was to be human! How different from being a fairy. Fairies are born of the forest, and the forest guides and protects them. They live their fairy lives, do their fairy work, and never suffer a moment of doubt. But humans must choose, and choosing is the highest honor and the heaviest burden in all the universe. The forest had begun the process of making Flora, but now that she was human, she would have to finish the job herself.

Flora may have been wrong to keep her promise to marry a man she did not love, but she knew of no other way to hold on to the memory of her lost Cor. So she chose to stay true to her promise; and the truth that lay at the heart of the world, the truth that had no beginning and will have no end, made its home inside her heart.

* * *

The days that led up to the wedding went by quickly, and the prince was more distracted than usual. The upcoming marriage was an important matter of state for the royal family. News of the wedding was spread abroad, and ships from all over the world poured into the harbor. Some of the ships brought ambassadors and foreign guests. Others brought magnificent gifts from kings and queens of other lands.

Whenever a ship was sighted, the prince wanted to know everything about it. He posted lookouts on the hills, so he would always be the first to hear of an approaching ship.

The night before the wedding Flora dreamed of Cor. He stood with his back to her, and although she called to him over and over, he would not turn to face her. She became angry, and blamed him for deserting her. She told him that he was a coward for leaving her all alone in the world of humans, and that he should be ashamed of himself. At last Cor turned, and stood before her, but she did not recognize his face.

Flora woke early the next morning. Her wedding gown lay on a sofa that stood near a large window. Flora picked it up, and tried to admire its beauty. Her eyes were blank as she turned the dress over in her hands. Just then, a shout came from the corridor outside her room.

"Flora, where are you? Oh, Flora, come quickly! It was

all true! Where are you, Flora?"

"I am here," Flora called out.

One of the bridesmaids came running into the room.

"What is the matter?" asked Flora.

"It was true, it was all true!"

"What was true?"

"The princess of Norvalia—the prince did promise to marry her! All the arrangements for the wedding had been made, when the prince left suddenly, saying his father was ill. News of his engagement to you has reached Norvalia, and a letter has arrived from the king saying his daughter has been insulted. He demands an explanation, or he says there will be war."

"Where is the prince?"

"No one can find him. Just after the letter arrived, a ship was seen leaving the harbor, and it's feared... Oh, Flora! Poor, poor Flora!"

The arrival of the letter, and the sudden disappearance of the prince, threw the palace into a state of confusion. It was agreed that the prince must be found, and compelled to keep his promise to the King of Norvalia's daughter. Norvalia's royal family was known for its temper, and even if it did not come to outright war, Norvalia would be a dangerous enemy.

With tears in her eyes the queen told Flora what had been decided. She feared that the news would break Flora's heart. The king told Flora that she might ask for anything, and if it was in his power to give, she would have it. Flora thanked the king and queen for their kindness, and asked only for their continued friendship. She wrote a note to the prince telling him that she bore him no ill will, and hoped for his future happiness.

The next day she left the palace.

Flora walked down the avenue that led to the palace gates, not knowing where she would go. She thought of her life as a fairy, when the years flowed by in perfect circles, and she thought of her life now, when every day was different, and everything mattered, whether she liked it or not.

Someone was waiting outside the palace gates. Flora recognized the young man she had seen near the edge of the forest.

"Where are you going?" he asked.

"I don't know," she answered. "I have nowhere to go."

"Then stay with me," he said.

"With you? But you are traveling the world, looking for someone to recognize you."

"That's all over now. You recognized me."

"When?"

"Just now."

"But that's because I saw you a only short time ago."

"That's good enough for me," said the young man. "Besides, I'm beginning to think I recognize you. Are you sure you don't know me?"

Flora looked into his eyes. She looked deeply, the way only a human can, and she wondered why she hadn't seen it before. But now she did see it, and Cor was holding her in his arms.

And so the young man ended his travels. He built a cottage that overlooked the harbor where the water sparkled and the king's ships spread their sails. When it was finished, Flora and Cor were married, and they lived together in the cottage just like ordinary people, if "ordinary" is a word that can be used to describe two people who are in love. Or really, to describe anyone who will never see the same day twice, and will wake each morning, and choose who to become.

One evening, the two lovers sat outside the cottage, watching the sun disappear beneath the golden waves. A breeze carried the smell of the ocean. Flora leaned her head on Cor's shoulder, and he turned to her and whispered,

"I will love you forever."

And she knew that it was true.

THE LITTLE CLOUD

High above the ground, there floated a little cloud. The cloud was happy living in the sky. The sky was clean and pure, and the only sound was the rushing of the winds. The cloud loved the winds. He loved the gentle winds from the south, that made him feel warm and sleepy. He loved the winds from the north, that were bracing and cold, and he loved the winds from the east, that were full of hope.

But the cloud wasn't always happy. He worried about the things on the ground far below. There was noise and confusion down there. Even though he was high in the air, he sometimes wondered if he was safe. On nights when there was no moon, he couldn't see the ground, and that frightened him. What if the ground things were rising? What if he was falling? The cloud didn't sleep well on nights when there was no moon.

Rain storms are when clouds fall to the ground. The little

cloud was afraid of getting caught in a rain storm. Sometimes all the clouds would rush together, and make the sky dark. They would shout, "Descend! Descend! Come with us, little cloud!" Their breath was hot, and they blew about making a terrible noise. The little cloud always ran away.

The cloud was watchful as he floated above the earth. He didn't hate the things he saw below, he only wanted them to stay away. He wished them well, and in his heart he tried to bless them. But his shadow glided over the ground, and left nothing behind.

One night, as the wind blew from the west, the cloud fell into a restless sleep. He dreamed he had fallen into a river, and was speeding toward a waterfall. He heard the crash of water on the rocks below. He awoke to find that he was traveling at a terrible speed. Dark clouds jostled him on every side. The air was filled with electricity and excitement.

"Help!" screamed the cloud.

He tried to escape the storm, but he couldn't fight the strong winds. The clouds surrounding him were shouting, and some flickered with lightening. There was no escape.

With a blinding flash of light and a peal of thunder, the little cloud fell to the earth.

He split into a thousand drops of rain, and landed in a forest. The forest floor was covered with fallen leaves, and beneath the leaves were tiny creatures who crept and crawled, and fed on the dead things of the forest. The cloud fell among these creatures, and he was afraid. The creatures drank the cloud, and began to move. They ate the dead things that lay on the forest floor, and made them clean. With the help of the cloud they made the dead things into food for the plants that grew there. The cloud fed the forest, and he was no longer afraid.

"I am life," said the cloud.

He sank deep into the earth, and into the roots of the trees. The roots pushed him upwards into the trunks and branches. The cloud filled the fibers of the living wood. The branches swayed in the in violence of the storm, but they did not break.

"I am strength," said the cloud.

When the sun rose, the cloud was waiting in the leaves of the trees. He was waiting to help catch the Children of the Sun. On they came, millions at a time, rushing through the air, faster than thought. They came without slowing down, their arms and legs like needles that pierced the cloud, and made him feel as if he were being unmade. A pang of fear shot through him, but he was too excited to care. The Children of the Sun danced madly with the cloud and the others who were with him in the leaves of the tree. When the dance was over, the Children of the Sun left behind the treasure they had been given at their birth, and filled the leaves with energy and life.

"I am power," said the cloud.

Deer came and ate the leaves. They drank the cloud from gurgling brooks that ran through the forest. The cloud laughed as he poured himself into their muscles. He felt the rhythm of their legs and the pounding of their hearts. The trees flashed by as the deer sprang through the woods. They leaped over streams that sparkled like diamonds.

"I am joy," said the cloud.

The little cloud was tired. He gathered himself together, and rose up into the air. The setting sun made the sky glow orange. The little cloud said nothing. He was peace.

THE APPLE TREE

There once was a beautiful princess who lived in a palace with her mother and father. Her eyes were like dark jewels, and her face was an ever-changing mirror of her soul, where curiosity and compassion, impatience and joy each took their turn, so that anyone who saw her found it hard to look away.

She was a young lady, the only child of the king and queen, and the nobles who visited the palace knew that whoever married her would one day rule the kingdom. But at state dinners and palace balls she sat beside her father, and any who approached her drew a look of royal disdain.

The princess didn't care for the court and its rituals. She loved to run among the winds of the gardens. She strolled for hours along paths that led through groves of pear trees, around splashing fountains, and down avenues of ancient elms. Her favorite place was a meadow that lay outside the palace grounds. It was full of grass and wildflowers. At the bottom of the meadow was a stream that gurgled over black rocks, and splashed down miniature waterfalls. The princess did not know how soon this beautiful place would bring to an end everything she cherished most.

The meadow belonged to a farmer who raised animals in his barns, and grew wheat in his fields. He rarely visited the meadow, because it was too hilly for plowing or building. So the grasses and wildflowers were left to grow as they saw fit.

The farm prospered, because the farmer loved his land. Each year he watched his labor rise from the ground in the form of healthy crops, and each year the land he worked became a little more like the perfect land in his imagination. He dug and built and sowed and plowed until his labor, his mind, and his soul intertwined with the land in mysterious ways. The farmer didn't think about it this way, though. He felt his muscles yearn for the weight of the plow, or his heart wish for a warmer stable for his horses, and he thought himself a very practical person.

The farmer had a son named Tom, who was not a practical person at all. He had curly hair, an easy smile, and a restless mind that dreamed of great deeds. He dreamed of danger, hardship, bravery, and poetry. Although he didn't love the farm the way his father did, Tom tried his best to be helpful. He wasn't afraid to volunteer for the most dangerous jobs, but although there was a great deal of work to be done, there wasn't much that was actually dangerous. So while he plowed the fields and fed the pigs, he pretended he was engaged in perilous quests, and sometimes drove the plow into a ditch, or fed the pigs the hay that was supposed to be for the horses.

The farmhouse had a large collection of books, mostly

sensible books written by men and women who were good and wise, but Tom's favorites were books of adventure. He read stories about knights-errant who fought fierce giants. He read about hard blows delivered to cruel enemies, and gentle courtesy toward those in need.

One of Tom's books was about a boy who mined diamonds deep in the earth, and had strange adventures in the caves he found there. Tom thought there must be diamonds beneath the farm, and he decided he would dig them up. It seemed like an excellent idea, but digging a diamond mine was harder work than Tom had expected. Nevertheless, spurred on by visions of sparkling gems and cave-dwelling monsters, he was determined not to give up.

Tom spent all his free time digging. As he worked, he built supports with wooden planks his father had given him so the dirt wouldn't slide back into the hole. In a few weeks he had dug a pit so deep he had to use a ladder to get in and out.

Then one day it began to rain. It rained all day long, and the ground became soaked with water. By the time Tom went in for dinner, he was completely covered with mud. That night the walls of the hole collapsed. If it had happened only a few hours earlier, Tom would have been buried alive. After that, his father put an end to diamond mining.

The loss of his diamond mine left Tom with nothing to do. He wandered the farm with his feet scraping the ground, but it was not long before his footsteps brought him to the meadow where the princess came each day. She was there, down by the stream, and despite the fact that he had never seen her before, Tom's keen eyes guessed at once who she was.

This was an adventure better than diamond mining. All the knights he had read about had great ladies whom they served. Here was an actual princess, right in his own backyard. Tom felt he must find some way of serving her, so he could earn the right to fall in love with her, and perhaps one day receive a glance from her eyes and a smile from her lips.

Tom paused, and scratched his head. Where to begin? The best way to introduce himself would be to rescue her from something, possibly a dragon, but where could he find a dragon? Last summer, Tom's mother had planted flowers in her garden that had attracted a pair of hummingbirds, and Tom wondered if there were any plants that attracted dragons.

For a moment it occurred to Tom that it wasn't completely fair to the dragon to entice it to the farm, and then slay it for the trouble it caused the princess, but Tom put that uncomfortable thought out of his mind. Besides, he didn't know of any plants that attracted dragons, and he was fairly sure they were meat-eaters, anyway.

Tom rubbed his forehead. He thought about tying up one of the pigs in the meadow as bait for a dragon, but then he realized that it wouldn't make much difference to a dragon whether the pig was in the meadow or in the sty. Since no dragons had shown any interest in the pigs so far, there probably weren't any in the neighborhood.

There had to be another way. Tom thought that rescuing the princess from pirates wouldn't be bad, but he faced the same problem with pirates that he did with dragons: none were conveniently available. Tom's spirits sank. Finding a princess had been a wonderful piece of luck, but making the most of it was proving to be more difficult than he had thought.

On most days, the princess spent the morning in the meadow, and then returned to the palace gardens to seek shelter when the sun became too hot. There were no trees in the meadow, and no shade for her to rest in. Tom wished she would stay. He hadn't yet figured out how he would introduce himself, but he thought about her from the moment he woke up in the morning until the time he fell asleep at night. The princess transformed the farm into a land of romantic adventure, but when she was gone, everything seemed twice as ordinary.

Then Tom thought of something he could do for her.

"I'll build a place for her to shelter from the sun when she gets tired," he said to himself. "Maybe then she will stay longer, and love the meadow even more."

Tom asked his father for some wood and some nails, but his father remembered the near disaster of the diamond mine, and warned Tom against any more construction projects. Tom begged him, but it was clear there would be no help from his father. Tom vowed he wouldn't give up.

One day, he saw a small man walking down the road, dressed as a peddler. Tom's sharp eyes told him this was no ordinary peddler. It was an imp. Imps are magical creatures, who are rarely seen, and they are often dangerous. Tom knew this, but the sight of the imp sent a thrill through his belly. He thought of the princess, and wondered if he might persuade the imp to help him.

The imp had been walking all day, and was covered with dust. Tom ran into the farmhouse, and came out a few minutes later with a plate of ham and bread in one hand, and a pitcher of foaming ale in the other.

Imps appreciate a good meal, but Tom should have known that it's a mistake to give an imp strong drink. They're unpredictable enough under ordinary circumstances.

"Good afternoon, sir," said Tom. "The day is hot, and the road is long. Won't you sit down, and refresh yourself with some food and drink?"

The imp was hungry, and with greedy hands, he accepted everything Tom gave him. Once the imp had settled himself by the side of the road, Tom decided it was time to take his chance.

"Sir," he said, "I can see you're no ordinary peddler, but rather one who possesses great power. I want to build a shady place in a sunny meadow, but I have no wood or nails. Will you help me?"

"No," said the imp, through a mouthful of ham. He was an ill-natured creature (as most imps are), and was annoyed at being interrupted just when he was beginning to enjoy his lunch. A moment before the ham had been delicious, but now he found it was dry. He drank deeply from the pitcher of ale.

"Have you ever heard of a thing called 'mustard'?" asked the imp.

"No," said Tom. Mustard wasn't common in that part of the kingdom.

"I thought not," said the imp, and he felt an urge to punch Tom in the nose. Maybe it had to do with the effects of the ale.

"Won't you help me?" asked Tom. "It's very important."

The imp gave Tom a sideways look. He had an idea.

"It isn't for a princess by any chance, is it?" asked the imp, who did, in fact, possess some magic.

Tom's face turned red.

"Yes," he admitted.

The imp squinted his eyes. He had already forgotten that it was Tom who had given him the lunch he was enjoying, and thought only about what a pest the boy was. He decided to play a trick on him.

"I'm no wizard," he said. "I can't make wood and nails appear out of thin air, but I'll do what I can for you, if you'll let me. My magic won't work unless you want it to. I can't help you build a shelter for the princess, but perhaps you can provide her with shade yourself. What do you think of that?"

"Even better," cried Tom. "I'll provide the shade, but how?"

"If you like, I think I might be able to turn you into a tree," said the imp.

"A tree! That doesn't sound right."

"No, I suppose it doesn't," said the imp, and he took

another long drink from the pitcher of ale. Then, wiping his mouth with his sleeve, he said,

"Of course, it would be a beautiful tree that the princess would love."

Tom thought about this. Maybe it would be a great adventure to be turned into a tree by a magical imp.

"But the tree will live only for a season," continued the imp. "Before the year is over it will wither and die."

"Wither and die? What will happen to me?"

"I don't know. It's all a great mystery. I'm not really that good at magic."

This was true. He wasn't much good at magic, and he had no idea what would happen to Tom at the end of the year. But he looked cunningly at Tom, and said,

"Besides, what do imps know about adventure? Or love. Now stop bothering me, and let me finish my lunch."

Tom thought about the beautiful princess, and in truth he was already half in love with her. He had given up on dragons and pirates, and he hadn't been able to think of anything else. He couldn't bear the thought of not being able to do something for her.

"Isn't there any other way you can help me?"

"No," said the imp. He stood up, brushed the crumbs off his clothes, and prepared to resume his journey.

"Wait, don't go. I'll do it. I'll become a tree."

There was a flash of light and a bang that echoed inside Tom's head, while the world turned upside down. When Tom regained his senses, it was dark, and the imp was gone. Tom got to his feet, and groaned. His body felt like it had been trampled by a dozen imps, and kicked by two dozen more. He examined himself. As far as he could tell, he hadn't suffered any serious injury. In fact, nothing had changed at all, no sign of magic. He made his way back to the farmhouse with an unsteady walk.

That night, Tom lay in bed, unable to sleep, asking himself whether the imp's magic would turn him into a tree that the princess would love, or whether it was only a joke. It was a question he couldn't answer, but neither could he stop asking. His thoughts went around and around.

The moon rose above the horizon, bathing the farm in its silver light. It shone through Tom's window, and his thoughts slowed down. With his face glowing pale in the moon's ghostly light, Tom fell into a deep sleep. He dreamed of the princess, and for the first time they stood face to face. He looked into her eyes, and his love for her grew.

The next morning, when Tom awoke, he discovered he had turned into an apple tree. Tom, the boy, had been whisked from his bed, plunged into the ground, and Tom, the apple tree, had sprung from the earth.

He didn't know it would happen so fast, so he didn't have time to say goodbye to his mother and father. His father thought Tom had run away to seek adventure, which was true in a way, despite the fact that Tom was firmly planted in the meadow behind the farmhouse.

But as Tom took stock of his new situation, he wasn't thinking about his mother and father. He was too full of excitement. His arms had become thick branches, and he reached them toward the sky with a mighty joy. His feet, which were now roots, sunk deep into the earth, and drew forth life-giving food from the meadow's rich soil. The sun shone overhead, and Tom knew that its beams would be strength and life. How delightful it would be to dine upon the pure light! But even though it was late spring, his branches were still bare, and Tom thought that he must wait a little.

Later that day the princess came to the meadow, and found that overnight a tree had sprung up on the hill that overlooked the stream.

"That's strange," she thought. She ran her hand down the rough bark. "It must be a magic tree."

That night, Tom exerted himself to the utmost of his strength, and in the morning, when the princess arrived, she saw the apple tree had been transformed into a cloud of white blossoms.

"Oh, how beautiful!" she cried.

A wind came out of the east, and the blossoms rained upon the princess like a downpour of fluttering light. She twirled with joy, laughing, until she fell to the ground on a carpet of white flowers. She looked up, and said,

"Thank you, dear tree."

The blossoms were now gone, and when the sun set, Tom again put forth all his strength. The next morning the princess found her tree covered with the lime-green leaves of springtime. Sunlight filtered through the leaves, making patterns of light and shadow ripple across her face. In the covering shade of the apple tree the princess imagined she was swimming beneath the sea. The waves overhead made the light dance, and the slow rhythm of the undersea plants lulled her to sleep.

All summer long the princess visited her beloved meadow with its apple tree on the hill. She walked among the wild flowers until she grew tired, and then lay down in the shade to rest. Sometimes she slept in the late afternoon, and felt as if she were held in a close embrace. She dreamed of a boy with curly hair and an easy smile. He seemed unable to speak, but he carried his soul in his eyes, and she thought she could understand what he wanted to say: *Don't worry, Princess. I'll protect you.*

And she laughed, because she was a princess, and didn't need to be protected. And the boy laughed, too, at his own foolishness. She thought she had never seen anyone so happy, and yet, at the same time, there was a shadow of sadness on his face, as if he were always saying goodbye.

When autumn came, the leaves turned gold, and apples ripened on the branches of the tree. The princess picked one, and bit into it. The apple was full of tastes that brought back memories of ancient autumn days full of golden sunshine. When she finished it, exhilaration flowed through her body. She could never eat more than one.

"I would die of happiness," she said to herself.

The princess loved her tree. She visited it as often as she could, but when autumn turned to winter, and the weather became cold, she spent less time in the meadow behind the farmhouse. The leaves fell off the tree, and it stood bare in the wind.

"Goodbye for now, dear tree," said the princess late one afternoon.

The first snow of winter was falling, and white flakes clung to the princess's eyelashes.

"I will see you in the spring, and we will be happy again."

The princess returned to the palace, and the apple tree was left alone in the gathering darkness. The next day it withered and died.

When winter came to an end the farmer decided to take a walk around his property to see what damage the wind and snow had done. He noticed the dead tree standing on the hill that overlooked the meadow.

"This tree is no good to anyone," he said to himself. "Perhaps I can find some use for it."

So he cut down the tree, and used the wood to build a fence for a new sty he had been thinking over in his mind during the winter.

It was not long before the princess came back to the meadow to once again fill her eyes with the beauty of her tree. When she reached the hill, and saw that the tree had been cut down, she couldn't breathe. She stared at the place where her tree used to grow, then blinded by tears, she ran from the meadow.

In the days that followed, the princess couldn't bear to go back. She sat in a chair, staring blankly, thinking about her apple tree. She remembered the summer afternoons when she had slept beneath its branches, and the boy she had seen in her dreams. She never dreamed about him now. She wondered who he was, and what had become of him.

* * *

The winter had been hard for poor Tom. When the apple tree died, and the princess stopped visiting him, he had become more and more miserable. He had been happy in the tree while it lived, but now he could no longer call it home. A dead tree is no place for the spirit of a living boy. Even so, he stayed as long as he could. The thought of having no body at all filled him with horror. And yet, to linger in the dead remains of the withered tree gave him such a feeling of revulsion, that it finally became unbearable. One night, when the moon hid itself behind wisps of ragged clouds, Tom tore himself from the dead branches, and found himself alone with a howling wind blowing through his soul.

All winter long Tom's spirit haunted the neighborhood of the dead tree, hoping that the princess would return. Thoughts of her filled his ghostly mind until he could think of nothing else. *Why doesn't she return?* He asked himself over and over, until it became the maddening refrain of a song that never ended. Tom remembered all he had done to make her happy, and his heart rebelled against the unfairness of it all. How could she forget him so easily? Why didn't she come back? If only he could see her face— see the look of love in her eyes—all would be well again. But day after day she did not come back, and his heart grew cold with resentment.

With no body to keep him warm, Tom froze during the

long winter nights. But the days were even worse. Each morning Tom thought that maybe today the princess would come back. But she never did. Again and again his hopes failed him, until he hated the dawning light of each new day. As love and hope deserted him, he became weak. The rays of the sun battered him with heavy blows, so he dove among the dead roots of the tree to hide until night.

In the darkness he wandered the meadow, following the paths the princess used to walk. But soon, his visits to the places where she had been no longer gave him comfort. The dead tree groaned as gusts of wind shook its empty branches, and even the pale light of the distant stars stung him like shards of falling glass. He said goodbye to all he had known, dove one last time among the roots of the tree, deeper than he had ever dove before, and he was gone.

* * *

The early spring was cold, but the brave snowdrops pushed their blossoms out of the wet earth, and brightened the palace gardens. The princess loved the eager flowers that held the promise of warm days ahead, but the songs of spring were absent this year. She wandered the palace, or sat staring into the fireplace at flames made pale by rays of sunlight that were not yet strong enough to warm the stone halls.

The princess's grandmother sat near her by the fire, knitting a scarf that would keep the princess warm when winter came again. Knitting by the fire, like any old woman in any house or cottage, was an unusual thing for the grandmother of a princess to do, but this grandmother was an unusual person.

"What's wrong?" she asked.

The princess looked up, and her eyes filled with tears. She told her grandmother the story of the apple tree she had loved and the boy she had dreamed about. When the princess finished, the old woman nodded, took her by the hand, and led her up a long winding staircase, up to the top of a tower that rose above the western side of the palace, where the grandmother had her bedroom. The room occupied the entire upper floor of the tower, so that if you looked out of the many windows, you could see all the surrounding countryside. Old books sat on shelves, while dark vines growing out of earthenware pots climbed the bookcases, wound their way around the legs of the furniture, and crept among papers scattered across the tables, until it was impossible to say whether the place was a bedroom, a library, or a jungle.

The princess's grandmother climbed a stepladder, pushed some vines aside, and removed a book that sat on a high shelf. Pressed between two pages was a yellow leaf. The princess took the leaf in her hand, and held it up to the sunshine that came in through the windows. At first she thought the leaf was made of gold, but it shone with a brighter light than any gold she had ever seen.

"Where did it come from?" asked the princess.

"It fell from your coat one afternoon. I had a feeling you might want it someday."

"Did it always shine like that?"

"No."

The princess's grandmother took the leaf, rolled it into a ball, and placed it in a cup. She lit a lamp, heated some water from a stone pitcher, and when the water was hot, she poured it into the cup with the leaf.

"Drink this," she said.

As the tart flavor of the tea washed over the princess's tongue, she thought of the first time she had seen the springtime leaves of her tree, and the light that had rippled and danced.

That night the princess dreamed she was in a dark room. As her eyes became accustomed to the gloom, she saw she was in a dungeon. On the floor sat a young man bound with chains. He raised his head to look at her, and at the moment their eyes met, the princess saw his expression transform. Love and joy swept across his face. She recognized him, and she understood the enchantment of her tree. The apple tree was gone, but the one whose love had brought it to life was here. She leaped forward to fall into his arms, but something held her back. Silvery chains, strong in spite of their delicacy, twined around her arms and legs. She cried out in despair, and woke up.

When morning came, the princess went to her grandmother's room, and told her about the dream.

"How can I help him?" she asked.

The old woman's face wrinkled in thought. She frowned. The more she thought, the deeper she frowned.

"Neither can help the other, if both are bound in

chains," she said.

"Grandmother, help me remove my chains."

The old woman shook her head.

"You don't know what you're asking. The chains you felt were the chains of a princess."

The princess looked down at her hands. On her finger was a silver ring her father had given to her. One side of the ring was imprinted with the king's royal seal. Since the day she had received it, no one had ever seen the princess without it. Now she took it off, and handed it to her grandmother.

"Help me remove the chains," she said.

The old woman looked at her granddaughter, searching her face for signs of doubt. Then, she unlocked a cabinet, and took out a brown glass jar. She measured out a teaspoon of faded flowers, and prepared a pale tea for the princess to drink. It tasted stale, and as she drank it, her arms and legs became like lead. A mirror hanging on the wall revealed an unfamiliar face. It no longer reflected the darting thoughts. It was heavy and still, like a pool of water that waits to be set in motion. She looked at her reflection for a long time, fighting down a lump in her throat. At last she thought: *He will recognize me.*

Her grandmother helped the princess remove her royal garments, and found clothes for her that were suitable for a servant. She took the princess down to the palace kitchen, and introduced her as the daughter of a peasant, a young woman looking for a job as a scullery maid. The princess was hired, and her grandmother held her close. The princess felt the warmth of her grandmother's lips on her forehead. Then, without saying a word, the old woman walked across the well-scrubbed floor, and closed the door behind her.

The work in the kitchen was hard. The princess could do only a small part of what the other servants did, and at the end of the day she fell into her bed, exhausted. Growing up in the palace, she had no opportunity of learning the ways of the kitchen, and knew almost nothing about the jobs she had to do. The other servants had to make up for the work she couldn't get done, and the princess wasn't popular.

Complaints about her became so frequent and so loud that at last she was dismissed from the kitchen. She was not quite thrown out to survive on her own, though. A farmer was looking for a girl to help with light work around his farm. He had recently lost a son, and there was no one else to help. One of the older matrons who worked in the kitchen felt sorry for the princess, so she recommended her for the job. The matron warned the farmer that the girl was stupid, though not lazy, and the farmer agreed to give her a try.

The princess arrived at the farm by the dusty road in front, rather than the meadow that lay at the back. She didn't know she had come to the house where Tom had lived.

It wasn't long before the princess was able to explore the farm, and soon she discovered where she was. Over dinner she heard stories about the farmer's son, who had dreamed of adventure, and suddenly disappeared. She questioned the farmer and his wife, and learned of the withered apple tree that had stood on the hill in the meadow, gone now, cut down to make a fence for the new sty.

The next morning the princess woke early, and hurried outside to examine the fence. She wondered if she could see Tom again in a dream, so she took a knife, and cut off a small piece of the wood. She used it to brew a tea as her grandmother had done with the golden leaf. That night she tossed and turned, anxious for the arrival of sleep, but when it came, it was dreamless.

Day after day, the princess stood by the sty, resting her arms on the railings of the fence, watching the pigs eat. She didn't know what to do.

* * *

Tom's ghost burrowed into the earth, seeking ever-deeper darkness. His only thought was to escape the light that burned, and the anger that gnawed in his throat. But his resentment was nourished by the darkness, and grew stronger. Tom no longer remembered why he had loved the princess. He thought only of how unfair everything was. Nothing mattered except that, and every moment was pain. Tom's soul was starving, but he knew of only one remedy: more darkness. Deeper and deeper he dove, until there was nowhere left to go. Tom came to the place of utter darkness, and there he stopped.

He looked around. He saw nothing. He looked inside himself. There was nothing there, either—no love, no longing, no pain. He wasn't even angry anymore. Why had he been so angry? In that place of nothingness it was hard to imagine anything important enough to be angry about. It was all foolishness and bother. Nothing was real, except the darkness.

"Now I know the deepest truth of all," thought Tom. "Nothing matters. Now, I'm free."

* * *

At first, the imp who had turned Tom into a tree gave little thought to the farmer's son. He continued on his travels, and soon was far away from the place where they had met. He had almost, but not quite, forgotten all about him. When he did remember, the thought made him feel uneasy, so he put it out of his mind. After a while, though, he began to feel sorry for what he had done. He wasn't a bad person, only ill-natured. Most imps are ill-natured, so it wasn't entirely his fault. He still felt bad, though. The thought of Tom ruined his dinner, his pipe after dinner, and his rest at night. So he decided to return to the farm to see if anything could be done.

When the imp arrived at the farm, he found the princess leaning against a wooden fence, and he gruffly wished her good morning. The princess looked down, and gave a jump when she realized she was being addressed by an imp.

"Maybe something's happening," she thought.

"Good morning, sir," she said carefully. "The day is hot and the road is long. May I get you something to refresh yourself with?"

The imp scowled at the princess. "What are you doing here?" he asked crossly. He wasn't fooled by her grandmother's disguise.

The princess blushed. She wasn't sure what to say.

"What are *you* doing here?" she countered.

The imp was about to give her a rude answer, but then he remembered why he *was* there, so he fought to control his temper.

"The boy's not in there," he said, pointing a stubby finger at the fence. "That wood's dead."

"I know," said the princess.

"Where is the boy, then?"

The princess looked hard at the imp. "Where is the boy, then?" she repeated.

The imp fidgeted, and cleared his throat several times. This princess had an uncomfortable way of looking at you, he thought. Finally, he sat down, lit a pipe, and unburdened himself by telling the princess the whole story about how he had turned Tom into an apple tree without quite knowing how things would end up. The princess told the imp about the dream she had after drinking the tea made from the golden leaf. They both sat in silence.

"Let me see what I can do," said the imp at last. He stood up, and without another word, he walked away.

The imp was gone for a long time. The princess was impatient for his return, but she never doubted that he would come back. As time went on, however, she began to wonder what difficulties he faced, and whether they could be overcome. One day, he finally returned. He looked at the princess, and frowned. Whenever the imp saw the princess, he felt twice as bad about what he had done to Tom.

"Come with me," he said.

"Will I be gone long?" asked the princess.

The imp gave a bitter laugh, and avoided the princess's eyes. She wrote a short note to the farmer, packed a few things in a bag, and said,

"I'm ready."

* * *

Tom wasn't sure how long he'd been in the darkness. There was nothing to mark the passing of time. It might have been a day, or it might have been a hundred years. All he knew was that he was lonely. He may have been a ghost who had reached the place of utter darkness, but he was still Tom. All around him was nothing, and nothing wasn't enough. He wanted more. But now that he was ready to leave, he realized that he didn't know the way out. He wasn't even sure if such a thing as a way out existed in that world of nothing.

His loneliness grew until it threatened to swallow him up. He searched the darkness for a glimmer of light. He strained to hear the tiniest sound that might hint at the presence of another person. He thought that even the feeling of pain would be better than the never-ending emptiness. But he had no body to feel pain.

Tom tried to remember his life before he became a ghost. He thought about his home, and he thought about the princess. That made him feel a little less lonely.

What had she been like? What had made him love her? For a long time Tom concentrated on these questions, when all of a sudden, she was there. Out of Tom's longing came an image of the princess that was as if she were standing right in front of him.

Tom looked at her, and he was ashamed. He saw her face, and he knew that the reason she hadn't come back was because she didn't know he needed her. If she had known, she would have come. If she had known, she would have gone to the very ends of the earth to find him. As the vision faded away, Tom looked into her eyes once more, and he thought that at that moment she did know.

A glimmer of hope awakened inside him, a spark of light that warmed rather than burned. It made him feel more steady, like a man who steps onto dry land after days of riding a stormy sea. In the midst of the murky darkness of nothing, he had found something solid to hold on to. The princess was on her way.

"I will be patient," he thought. "This time, I will trust her."

Tom took a deep breath, and sat down. He stared into the darkness, wondering if it was a little less dark than before. The place where he sat felt uncomfortable, and all of a sudden Tom realized he had a body again. He gave a shout, and jumped up, but he couldn't move more than a few feet. His arms and legs were bound by chains. Tom pulled at them with all his strength, but the chains held firm. On the verge of being overcome by despair, Tom stopped himself.

"At least I'm no longer a ghost," he thought. "It's a start."

* * *

The princess didn't know where the imp was taking her, and sometimes she thought the road they traveled would never end. They followed paths that crisscrossed up mountains higher than any the princess had ever seen. As they climbed, she thought,

"We will find him at the top of the highest mountain."

But when they reached the top, they continued down the other side, and the princess knew their journey wasn't over. Sometimes they traveled through thick forests, and the princess thought,

"He must be at the center of the thickest forest in the world."

But the imp's strong legs kept going, step-after-step-after-step, and it seemed as if their journey would never end.

At last they reached a forest that was darker than any they had traveled through before.

"Where are we?" the princess asked.

"Shh," whispered the imp.

The air was damp. All was silent except for the sound of the two travelers as they walked over wet leaves, crushing rotting sticks beneath their feet. They went on for a long time, deep into the forest, until they came to a small building made entirely of stone. Its roof was a single slab of rock, no higher than the top of the princess's head. The stones that made up the walls were roughly cut, and covered with dark stains. The air around the building was so cold that the princess could see her breath. There were no windows, only a heavy door.

"Let us go away from this place," whispered the princess.

"Open the door," said the imp.

"No, I cannot."

"You must."

The handle of the door made the princess's hand burn with cold. She turned it, and pulled the door open. Inside she saw solid darkness—as solid as the stones that framed the door. The princess stared at the darkness, her feet glued to the ground, the forest spinning around her. She cried out, and would have fallen if the imp hadn't caught her, and pulled her away from the door. She sank to the ground with her back against a tree, and hid her face between her hands.

The imp picked up a handful of stones and threw them toward the door. They disappeared as they reached the wall of darkness. He listened for the sound of the stones hitting the ground, but no sound came. The imp picked up a stick and poked it into the darkness. No part of the stick that entered the darkness came out. It was as if the stick had been broken off, and the place where it broke was frosted with ice.

"Your path lies through that door, Princess," said the imp.

"No. I will do whatever I have to, but I cannot pass

through that door. You must find some other way."

"There is no other way. If you will not go this way, then our journey is over."

"Will you go with me?"

"No."

"Why not?"

"I cannot," said the imp.

The princess looked into the darkness.

"Will I find him through that door?" she asked.

"You will find something."

The princess stood up. She thought of the young man with the curly hair and the easy smile. She took a deep breath, closed her eyes, and walked through the door.

The imp watched as the girl disappeared into the darkness.

* * *

It was cold, and for a moment the princess couldn't breathe. She couldn't see her arms or legs. Her whole body felt numb, and she was afraid. She wondered if she was dead, but the princess was a sensible person, as all true princesses are, and she said to herself,

"If I'm afraid, then I must be alive. I will go and find Tom."

She started to walk, and soon she felt a little warmer. After a while her eyes became accustomed to the dark, and she could see the floor, which was made of dirt, and a little way in front of her. She couldn't see as far as the walls on either side, and she imagined rough stones covered with dark stains. She shuddered.

The cave, or tunnel, or prison, the princess didn't know which, was silent. Her feet made no sound on the hard-packed floor. She walked for what seemed liked miles, unable to tell how far she had traveled, or how long she had been in the darkness.

Then a sound reached her ears. She moved forward slowly. On the ground was the dim outline of a body. She drew in her breath as the body began to move. It looked up, and she saw that it was a young man. His face was sad, but as he looked at her, the sadness faded away, and was replaced by an expression of perfect happiness. The princess forgot she was in a dark prison. The smile on the young man's face was like sunshine on a summer day.

Tom gazed at the princess who had searched for him and found him. Now, at last, he was truly free. What difference did it make whether he was in a dark prison or a bright meadow? *She* was with him. He looked down at his chains as if to say *What do I care about you now!* But they were gone. He rose to his feet, somewhat stiffly, and bowed.

"Good evening, Princess," he said. "Thank you for coming."

"Thank you for inviting me," she said with a laugh, and kissed him.

They walked together through the darkness without knowing or caring where they went. They had a thousand things to tell each other. After a while the princess felt the wind in her hair, and looking up, she saw the moon and stars gleaming high above her head. Tom didn't notice. He was too busy telling her about the time he first realized he was in love with her. The princess smiled, and her face reflected the darting thoughts that danced through her head. She was herself again. Perhaps the door of darkness had taken away her grandmother's spell, or maybe it was the way Tom looked at her, or maybe the spell wasn't needed anymore, and had enough sense to leave on its own.

They found the imp still sitting in front of the doorway, staring into the darkness. Tom closed the door, and turned to the imp.

"Of all the foul, nasty creatures I have ever met," he began. But the princess whispered something in Tom's ear, and he bit his lip.

"Shake," he said, holding out his hand.

"Apology accepted," said the imp.

* * *

Early the next year, a crumpled package arrived at the palace. There was a note attached to it.

I have better things to do than attend weddings, so don't bother sending me an invitation.

At the bottom of the note were the words, *Address All Correspondence To:* followed by the imp's address, printed carefully.

Inside the box was an apple, shimmering with light. The princess and Tom planted it in the meadow that lay behind the farmhouse. The next day a tiny sprout poked through the earth, and soon a tall tree spread its branches over the hill.

When summer came, the princess and Tom were married. They stood together beneath the apple tree, and placed golden rings on each other's fingers. The branches of the tree, weighed down by clusters of leaves, surrounded the two lovers, as if protecting them.

After all the words had been spoken, and everyone went away, they remained together on the hill. The leaves fluttered on the tree. Ever-changing patterns of light and shadow danced across their faces, and each found it hard to look away.

.

AVERY AND SOPHIE

In a village near the edge of a peaceful kingdom there stood an ancient water mill. Outside the mill a wooden wheel rolled in the current of a stream, while inside creaking gears pushed a heavy stone around in a circle, making a noise like thunder. Farmers brought their wheat to the mill, and the stone crushed the wheat into flour, which was used to bake bread for all the people in the village.

A miller and his son lived there—in a loft near the ceiling, surrounded by turning gears, high above the rumbling stone. The son's name was Avery. He was a fine looking boy, but he was always covered in cuts and bruises. That was Sophie's fault.

Sophie and Avery had been friends for as long as they could remember, and they did everything together. They played the same games, they sang the same songs, and yet, in one way they were very different. Avery was said to be the most handsome boy in the whole village, but no one had ever called Sophie a beauty. They said she was "plain." Avery didn't notice, though, because whenever he saw her, he felt happy. Sophie had that effect on everyone.

One day, Sophie came running up to Avery as he was coming out of the mill, and shouted,

"I found the tallest tree in the world. Do you think you can climb it?"

Avery was an excellent tree-climber.

"Show me where it is," he said.

Sophie led him to the tree she had found. They stood in front of it, and Avery tipped his head back as far as it would go.

"Can you climb it?" asked Sophie.

"It's not much of a climbing tree," said Avery. "Look how far apart the branches are."

"You'll have to jump from branch to branch like a squirrel!" said Sophie, clapping her hands together.

Avery wasn't sure about jumping from branch to branch like a squirrel, but Sophie seemed to think he could do it, so he thought he probably could.

He couldn't.

At first, he found some branches that were not too far apart. By balancing carefully on the lower branch, he could stretch up, get his hands around the higher one, loop one leg over it, and pull himself up. But when it came time to make his first leap toward a branch that was farther away, he hesitated.

Sophie was directly below him, her eyes wide, as she held

her breath. Avery bent his knees, judged the distance, and jumped. He flew through the air, his arms extended in front of him. He grabbed at the approaching branch, and the rough bark scraped across his skin. His hands slid over the surface, but he couldn't hold on. He lost his grip, and plummeted to the ground.

Sophie rushed over to him.

"Oh, Avery, I'm so sorry!" she said, as she wiped the blood from his arms and legs. "I never should have told you to do it."

It wasn't the first time Sophie's confidence in Avery had resulted in disaster, and it wasn't unusual for Sophie to find herself washing off his cuts, and crying over his bruises. Avery groaned, and Sophie promised herself that she would never again tell him about tall trees, or mention heroic leaps across streams full of slippery rocks. But it was hard to remember.

The next day, in order to show how sorry she was, Sophie made a picnic lunch. They walked across a meadow, and Sophie laid a red and white checkered cloth under the branches of a shady tree. She unpacked chicken salad, a loaf of bread, sliced cucumbers, and raspberry cream cake for dessert.

Sophie divided up the food, making sure Avery got the bigger portion of everything. It looked delicious, and Avery dug in right away. It was a remarkable thing to see him eat. He barely chewed, as great lumps of food disappeared down his throat. Sophie watched with her mouth open. She hadn't made nearly enough.

A few moments later, Avery's lunch was gone. He smacked his lips, and looked around with raised eyebrows. He noticed the untouched food on Sophie's side of the red and white cloth.

"You take it," she said.

"But that's yours," said Avery.

"It's all right. It fills me up just watching you eat."

"Really?" asked Avery.

"Really," said Sophie.

So Avery ate Sophie's lunch, and thought it was a lucky thing that girls could get full by watching boys eat.

* * *

Avery and Sophie grew up together, and the day came when they were no longer children. Avery had become a young man, and he decided it was time to get married, so he asked Sophie for her advice. She wrinkled her brow. The question was an important one, and Sophie said she would give it some thought.

Sophie was in love with Avery, but she never thought of marrying him herself. Sophie's mirror told her she wasn't beautiful, and she thought that only the most beautiful woman in the world would be good enough for Avery. Of course, Sophie's mirror was wrong. The problem was that Sophie's beauty lay in her heart, and although Avery had become a young man and she a young woman, neither one was old enough to see the things that are invisible.

After thinking it over for a few days, Sophie decided that

Avery should marry Princess Snowflake, who lived on the other side of the kingdom. She was said to be the most beautiful princess in the world, and whoever married her would be king. So that was another point in her favor. Avery agreed this was an excellent idea, and he decided he would travel to the royal palace without delay.

It was all very sudden, and the thought of losing the friend she had known all her life made Sophie feel sad. So she went to her room, opened a drawer in a wooden chest, dug down to the bottom, and removed a small bag that clinked with the sound of silver coins. Sophie took the bag to the market, and returned later in the afternoon carrying an armful of packages.

"I got you some things for your journey," she said to Avery.

"Did you really? Did you get me a sword?"

"Oh, Avery, I didn't think to buy a sword," said Sophie. Then she turned pale. "You don't think you'll be doing any fighting, do you?"

"Well, you never know," said Avery. "And it's always best to be prepared."

Sophie unwrapped the packages, and handed Avery a soft, white shirt, a woolen coat, and a pair of boots. The boots had strong leather sides that came up to Avery's ankles, and thick, black soles. They were magnificent boots. They were the kind of boots that make your legs yearn for the open road.

Avery put the boots on. They fit perfectly, and he took a step. The heel touched the ground, and the boot rolled forward to the toe. He took a few more steps. Heel-toe, heel-toe, the boots rolled forward like twin ships plowing through the sea.

"Where are you going?" called Sophie.

Avery turned and shouted, "I don't know. I'll be back later. I'm trying out the boots. They're very good."

Avery woke early the next morning, packed a few things, and said goodbye to his father. Sophie was waiting for him outside the mill.

"Will you take this, Avery," she said, "and think of me sometimes?"

It was a white handkerchief. Avery thanked Sophie for the gift, and put it in his pocket. Then Sophie began to cry, so he took it out again, and used it to dry her tears. Sophie kissed him tenderly, and watched as he disappeared into the distance.

* * *

The road was good, the sky was filled with sunshine and bright clouds, and soon Avery was far from the village where he had lived his whole life. He passed fields, orchards, and streams. At night he slept on soft grass, and every morning he woke happy and refreshed. His first thought as he opened his eyes was, *I wonder what Sophie and I will do today.* But then he remembered that Sophie was far away, and it became, *I wonder what Sophie will do today.*

Each day brought him closer to the palace, and Avery wondered what it would be like to marry a princess. Surely, it would be grand, he thought. But maybe the princess wouldn't like him, and then he'd have to go back to the village. That would be uncomfortable. And yet, if that happened, he'd see Sophie again.

One day, as Avery walked along the road, he heard shouts coming from behind a farmhouse. He ran up the drive to see what was the matter, and found a small creature, no more than three feet tall, chained with an iron shackle to a large rock that stuck out of the ground. The creature looked like a small a man with short legs, short arms, and a wrinkled face.

"Ouch! Ouch!" yelled the creature.

"Stop your screaming," said Avery. "What's the matter?"

"Set me free! Set me free!"

"Why don't you set yourself free, Gremlin?"

"I'm no gremlin. I'm the King of the Fairy Goblins."

"Well then, why don't you set yourself free, King of the Fairy Goblins? What good is it being a fairy goblin, if you have no magic? And what's the good of having magic, if you can't get yourself free from an iron chain?"

"You blockhead! Don't you know the fairy folk can't stand the touch of cold iron? If it doesn't come off, it will kill me."

"How long has it been on?" asked Avery.

"A year and a day," said the fairy goblin.

"Well, if it hasn't killed you yet, I don't think it will kill you at all. I have to go. I'm going to marry Princess Snowflake, and if I don't hurry, someone else might marry her first."

"Help, help, set me free!" shouted the fairy goblin.

"Why are you chained up, anyway?"

"The farmer thinks that having a fairy goblin on his farm will make his corn grow faster."

"Does it?" asked Avery.

"Of course not!" said the fairy goblin.

"Then why doesn't he let you go?"

"Because he thinks it does. Every morning he comes out, cocks his head at the corn, and rubs his hands together. But the corn is exactly the same height as it was last year."

"Still," said Avery, "it must be a source of comfort for him to be able to say that the King of the Fairy Goblins is chained up in his yard. It probably makes his neighbors respect him."

"Yes, I imagine you're right," said the fairy goblin, becoming more calm. "I can see that."

"I'd like to help you," said Avery, "but I don't see how I can. I don't have a file, a saw, or anything else that can cut through iron."

"What do you have?"

"Half a loaf of bread and a lady's handkerchief."

"Give them to me."

The fairy goblin took a bite from the loaf of bread, and spit it out.

"Terrible," he said.

Then he looked at the handkerchief, and said *hmmm, hmmm*. He handed it back to Avery.

"This is a good handkerchief," he said. "Rub the iron chain with it. It should work quite well."

Avery rubbed the iron chain with Sophie's handkerchief, but nothing happened.

"I don't think it's working," he said.

"Keep rubbing, boy. Don't give up so easily."

Avery rubbed some more. Nothing happened.

"I don't think I can rub through an iron chain with a handkerchief," he said.

"Let me look."

The fairy goblin looked at the place where Avery had been rubbing. He moved closer and closer until his nose was almost touching the chain.

"Not quite," he said. "Just a little more to go."

"Just a little more to go? The handkerchief has done nothing."

The fairy goblin looked again. He put his face right up to the chain, and made more *hmmm hmmm* noises.

"Just a little more to go," he repeated. "Keep at it."

So Avery kept at it. He worked day and night. When the farmer came to look at the corn, Avery hid behind a bush, and when the farmer left, he went back to work, trying to rub his way through the iron chain with the handkerchief Sophie had given him.

Every evening the subjects of the King of the Fairy Goblins, led by the Prime Minister, brought him his dinner. They were careful to keep away from the iron chain. They brought their king boar's fat soup, roasted onions, and a salty cheese made from goat's milk. They generally brought nothing for Avery. Once in a while, they remembered Avery might be hungry, so they gave him a raw turnip. Fairy goblins know little about what humans like to eat, and when Avery tried to explain it to them, they stuck their fingers in their ears, and said *La, la, la, la, la, la, la.*

Working on the iron chain all day was dull work, and Avery had a lot of time to think. He thought mainly about Sophie. Avery missed her, and although he didn't seem to be getting any closer to freeing the fairy goblin, he kept at it. He thought that was what Sophie would do. He kept at it for months.

Back in the village, Sophie missed Avery, too. Her face wasn't as bright as it used to be, and she ate little. The cold weather came, and while Avery rubbed the iron chain in the falling snow, Sophie grew thin, and then became sick. One day she got into bed, and never left it until her still body was carried to the churchyard, and laid to rest in the ground.

That evening, the fairy goblin's Prime Minister whispered the sad news in the king's ear. The fairy goblin told Avery what had happened in tones more gentle than one would have thought him capable of. Avery said nothing. He rubbed the iron chain harder than ever, and Sophie's handkerchief became damp with his tears.

The day finally came when Avery freed the King of the Fairy Goblins. The snows had melted and spring had come. The break of day found Avery already at his work. As the sun rose above the roof of the farmhouse, Avery felt the warmth of its rays on his skin.

The fairy goblin yawned, stretched out his arms, and rubbed his eyes with his fists. All of a sudden there was a bang, and the chain fell to pieces in Avery's hands. He shook them, and grimaced. His hands stung as if he had been chopping wood, and had hit a hard knot. Pieces of broken metal lay all around him, and the fairy goblin was gone.

Avery stood up, brushed himself off, and wondered what to do next. He had been looking forward to the day when his work would be done, but working on the chain had at least given him something to do. It had helped him avoid sad thoughts, thoughts that had made his chest ache and his throat feel tight.

Avery's first idea was to return to the village to see Sophie's grave. He closed his eyes, and imagined what it would look like. It wasn't very interesting, so he decided to do something else. He now understood that he shouldn't have left the village. But since Sophie was gone, he thought he might as well continue his journey to the palace of Princess Snowflake. The princess wasn't Sophie, but she was said to be beautiful, and at this point that was probably the best he could do.

Avery gathered his belongings together, walked back to the road, and once again set off on his journey.

* * *

When Avery arrived at the palace, he introduced himself, and explained why he had come. The palace guards didn't think much of a miller's son, but they carried his message to the princess, and she agreed to see him.

"Follow me," said one of the guards.

Avery was led down a long corridor where the floor was covered with thick carpet, and the ceiling was inset with gold. The corridor led to a lofty gallery with a marble floor and statues on pedestals. The distant ceiling was a dome of frosted glass. Beyond the gallery was an open courtyard where doves scattered in clouds of beating wings. At last they reached the throne room of Princess Snowflake.

The room was so brightly lit that Avery had to put his arm in front of his face to protect his eyes from the glare. The room was vast. Avery couldn't see where it ended, and he wondered if it went on for miles. White velvet quilts covered the floor. In some places they were piled as high as Avery's head, which gave the room a hilly appearance.

Flashes of light caught Avery's eye. He looked up, and saw dozens of crystal ornaments. Their spiky points hovered motionless above his head, and Avery was afraid to breathe lest the tiniest puff of air should disturb their icy perfection.

Princess Snowflake sat on the throne. She was dressed all in white, from the silk slippers on her feet to the diamonds in her hair. She wasn't as tall as Avery had expected, but she was even more beautiful than her fame had promised. Avery approached the throne, and bowed.

Princess Snowflake looked at the miller's son, and smiled. She buried her tiny feet beneath the thick blankets that lay at the foot of the throne, and hugged herself. This young man's looks were truly charming, she thought, and his visit to the palace was the happiest thing that had happened all day.

Avery saw the smile, and moved closer.

"Good morning, Princess," he said. "My name is Avery. I'm the son of a miller who lives on the other side of your kingdom."

"Good morning, Avery," she said. "Welcome to my palace. I'm glad that you have come. What gift have you brought me?"

Avery's face fell. He hadn't thought of bringing a gift, and he had nothing to offer the princess. He tried to think of something to say.

"I... I didn't know Your Highness's taste," he stammered. "I thought it would be a shame if I brought you something you wouldn't like."

The princess smiled again.

"Your thoughtfulness," she said, "means more to me than all the riches that have been scattered at my feet. Some have tried to win my heart with chests of gold that took a thousand men to carry, while others brought barrels filled with rubies, each the size of an ostrich egg, but none has ever stopped to ask after my own taste. Do you know that I care nothing for rubies or gold? What my heart longs for is the beauty of a single flower."

While the princess had been describing the rich gifts of her other suitors, Avery had shoved his hands in his pockets, and kicked the ground with his toe, but when she mentioned the flower, his face brightened.

"I will get you a flower," he said.

"Will you?" said the princess. "As soon as I saw you, I could tell that you were different, that you were one who cared only for my happiness."

"Yes—that's true, I think" said Avery.

"The flower I want," said Princess Snowflake, "is the Pallid Antrosis that grows in the Pit of Black Despair. The pit is guarded by the three-headed Serpent of the Abyss. No man has ever faced the serpent, and returned alive."

"The pallid what?" asked Avery.

"The fangs of the serpent are like daggers, and each neck is a hundred feet long," continued the princess. "It attacks with one head, and when a man raises his sword to parry the jaws of death, the other two heads slice his body from either side, so that no battle against the beast has ever lasted for more than three seconds."

A few moments ago the possibility of obtaining chests of gold or barrels of rubies had seemed remote. Now, however, treasuring hunting was looking more and more appealing. But the diamonds in the princess's hair sparkled, and her smile made Avery feel that anything was possible. So he decided he would get the princess the flower she wanted, or die trying.

"If I am to battle the triple-headed serpent, Princess, I will need a worthy weapon," said Avery. "I have no sword of my own. Will you lend me one?"

"I can't," said the princess. "I don't have one, either."

"But, Princess! On the way to the throne room I passed your royal armory. It's as big as a farmer's field, and it's filled with the finest weapons I have ever seen in my life!"

"Yes, but I might need those," said the princess. "I'm so sorry."

"That's all right," Avery mumbled. "I understand."

Avery asked the gentlemen of the court if any of them would lend him a sword, but they all refused. They were shocked that Princess Snowflake would give a miller's son a chance to win her heart. They could see how handsome Avery was, and they feared that if he succeeded in returning with the Pallid Antrosis, he would become the princess's favorite. Besides, the princess had given each of them a great task, but none had been brave enough to try. That made them hate Avery even more.

So in the end, Avery set out on his quest empty-handed.

Although he had no sword, Avery had the good boots Sophie had given him, and he reached the Pit of Black Despair in a few days' time. The entrance to the pit was a cave that was partially hidden by bushes and weeds. Avery ducked down, and stepped inside.

Shafts of light pierced the darkness of the cave where the ceiling had crumbled away. The walls were made of brown rock, and piles of flat, jagged stones covered the floor. The path wound its way through the cave, and Avery moved slowly, stopping to look around each corner. He didn't want to stumble on the three-headed serpent without knowing it.

No sound reached Avery's ears except the crunching of his own boots on the shards of rock. The cave went on and on. He saw no flower and no serpent. Avery was beginning to wonder if the princess had given him the wrong directions, when he heard a faint scraping noise ahead of him. It wasn't like the crunching his boots made. It was quieter, like the sound of sand pouring through an hourglass. Avery stuck his head around the corner, and looked.

He saw a large space, like a great hall or a cathedral. The Pallid Antrosis lay in the center, growing out of the rocky ground. It was illuminated by a beam of light that fell from the ceiling high above Avery's head. The flower was white, with four broad petals surrounding a central disk that was pale yellow, like custard.

Around the Pallid Antrosis slithered the serpent, it's three heads drew wavy lines among the broken stones.

Now what? thought Avery, and then he saw the King of the Fairy Goblins standing at his side.

"What are you doing here?" whispered Avery.

"You freed me from the cold iron," said the fairy goblin in a soft voice, "so I've come to help you."

"I told Princess Snowflake I'd bring her that flower," said Avery, pointing toward the Pallid Antrosis. "But I don't know what to do about the serpent."

The fairy goblin narrowed his eyes as he looked at the serpent. He stroked his chin.

"It's got three heads," he said.

"I know," said Avery.

"You don't see that very often," said the fairy goblin.

"Yes, but how can I get the flower?"

"You'll have to do something about the serpent first," said the fairy goblin.

"Yes, I know!" said Avery, breathing hard, and looking around, as if hoping to find some other source of help. Unfortunately, except for the serpent, there was no one else in the cave.

"Have you got a sword, by any chance?" asked Avery.

"Let me check," said the fairy goblin.

He searched in his pockets, and found three pebbles and a stick.

"I had forgotten about these," he said.

"What are they?" asked Avery.

"Three pebbles and a stick," said the fairy goblin.

"Yes, I know, but what are they for?"

"You could throw one at the serpent."

"What would that do?" asked Avery.

"The pebbles are magic," said the fairy goblin.

"What about the stick?"

"It's just an ordinary stick."

"I'll take a pebble," said Avery.

"Are you sure?" asked the fairy goblin.

"Of course I'm sure," said Avery.

The fairy goblin handed Avery a pebble, and Avery threw it at one of the heads of the serpent. He had good aim. The pebble hit the serpent right between the eyes, and bounced lightly to the ground.

The serpent turned toward Avery, and tipped its head to one side. It hadn't noticed Avery before, and it wasn't sure what to make of him. No one had ever attacked it with a small pebble before. The serpent looked at the pebble and sniffed it. It gave the pebble a push with its nose. The pebble rolled a few inches. The serpent looked at Avery, then it looked at the pebble, then it looked at Avery again. It was having trouble making sense of it all.

Then something strange happened. The serpent began to move more slowly. It stretched out its neck toward Avery, but it was as if the serpent were moving through syrup. The muscles in its neck bulged as it fought to reach Avery with its teeth. But it couldn't. It moved more and more slowly until finally it stopped, frozen in place, no more than an arm's length from where Avery stood. The freezing process happened in the same way with the other two heads, and now the entire serpent was completely immobile.

Avery ran to the center of the cavern, dug with his hands around the roots of the flower, and lifted it out of the ground. He wrapped it in a cloth, and ran back to where he and the fairy goblin had been standing, but no one was there. The fairy goblin had disappeared. Avery put the flower in his pack, and returned to the palace.

* * *

"Truly, Avery, there is no one like you in all my kingdom," said Princess Snowflake, as she took the Pallid Antrosis from Avery's hands. "No one has ever faced the three-headed serpent and survived. Now I see that I have been deceived. You are no miller's son at all, but rather a great prince in disguise."

"No I'm not," said Avery.

But the princess continued as if Avery hadn't spoken.

"I know what will happen next. First you will make me fall in love with you, and then you will carry me off to your kingdom, far away from my home. Once we are married, you will insist on everything being done your way, and I won't even get to choose what I eat for my dinner!"

The princess began to cry.

"That's not true," said Avery. "We can stay here in your palace, and you can eat whatever you want."

"Do you know what I would like?" said the princess, wiping her tears. "I would like to have just one bite of the Gentle Bluefish that swims in the River of Peaceful Waves. Will you get it for me?"

"Is there a serpent?" asked Avery.

"No."

"Then I'll try."

"It's a long journey to the land where the Gentle Bluefish lives," said the princess, "and when you reach the River of Peaceful Waves, you must be careful, because the water is poison. One drop can kill an entire army."

"That doesn't sound very peaceful," said Avery.

"And you must take care when you see the Gentle Bluefish itself. It has teeth like razors, and it can leap into the air and fly. It's powerful jaws tear the arms off of anyone who comes too close. And it's as fast as lightning."

"I don't think that fish is well named."

"Perhaps not, but the flavor is delicious when it's cooked just right, and I cannot consent to marry you unless you bring me one for my dinner," said the princess."

"I will try," said Avery, and he wondered what kind of wife the princess would make.

Princess Snowflake snuggled deep into the cushions of her throne, and thought about the wonderful fish. She put the Pallid Antrosis to her nose, and breathed its perfume. She was becoming fond of Avery, so instead of sending him out empty-handed, as she had done when he went to fight the serpent, she gave him a net with a long handle that he could use to catch the Gentle Bluefish.

Avery looked at the net. It was made of string.

"Do you think the net will be strong enough to resist the razor teeth of the fish?" he asked.

"No," said the princess.

Avery walked for eight days to reach the River of Peaceful Waves. It was full of pointed rocks, and the rushing water frothed white as it crashed against their edges. Poisonous spray flew in all directions so that Avery couldn't get within twenty paces of the water for fear of being splashed.

Suddenly a fish with bulging eyes and enormous jaws broke from the surface of the water, hovering in mid-air. The fish saw Avery, and with a whirring noise, it flew straight for the place where Avery's right arm was attached to his shoulder. Avery jumped out of the way of the flashing teeth, and the Bluefish flew back into the water. Avery scrambled behind a rock to protect himself from further attack.

He looked at the fragile net the princess had given him. He couldn't get close enough to the water to use it, and even if he could, the fish would chew right through it. Avery sat down, and wondered what to do. Should he return to the palace with no fish? Should he go back home, so he wouldn't have to admit his failure to the princess?

Maybe he should just let the fish tear him to pieces.

Then he noticed that the fairy goblin was once again standing at his side.

"It's you!" he cried. "Have you come to help me?"

"Of course I have."

"Did you bring the magic pebbles?"

"No. Today I only brought the stick."

"Show me."

The fairy goblin emptied his pockets onto the ground. There were two pebbles and a stick.

"You do have the magic pebbles."

"I suppose I do. But still, I recommend the stick."

"Is it a magic stick?"

"No."

"A special stick?"

"No, just an ordinary stick," said the fairy goblin.

"In that case, I'll take a pebble," said Avery.

Just then, a whirring noise filled the air. The fish had discovered where Avery was hiding, and had come to tear off his arms. Avery picked up a pebble, and threw it at the fish. He aimed well, and the pebble bounced off the head of the fish with a sharp "tock."

The same thing happened to the fish that had happened to the three-headed serpent. It moved slower and slower until it stopped, suspended in mid-air. Avery gripped the net, and swung. The fish tried to bite through the strings, but its jaws were stuck, and it did no more damage than an old man with nothing in his mouth but gums. Avery dumped the fish into his pack, and returned to the palace.

* * *

"I've brought you your fish, Princess," said Avery, walking into the throne room.

"Have you really? You are so kind, Avery," sighed Princess Snowflake. "I hardly know what to say."

"Well… I was hoping we could get married," said Avery.

The princess yawned.

"There's nothing in the world that would make me happier," she said.

There was a pause.

"Yes?" said Avery.

"But it's so hard being a princess. How can I think of marriage with the way things are? If only they were different!"

"Different?"

"Yes."

Avery scratched his thigh.

"Do I have to make things different?"

"Would you? I didn't want to mention it after all you've done, but there's an awful giant who's been causing so much trouble. He has a flaming sword, and knocks down trees in the royal forest. He murders villagers, and frightens the deer. It would be such a help if you would kill him, and bring me his head."

"Bring you the head of a giant!"

"He's not that big—thirty or forty feet at most."

"That's very big for me."

"I wouldn't ask you if any of the other knights could do it. But all the brave ones are dead. You're not afraid, are you?"

"It's hard to say," said Avery. "I don't have much experience with giants. Maybe we could get married first, and I could practice on some smaller giants, and then, after a while, I could try the big one."

"But I don't have any smaller giants," said the princess. "He's the only one."

"I see," said Avery.

There was a pause.

"Then I suppose it can't be helped," said Avery.

"No," said the princess. "I wish there were some other way. But there isn't."

Avery couldn't think of anything else to say, so he said goodbye to the princess, and set out on his journey to seek the giant.

When Avery came to the forest where the giant lived, fallen trees everywhere testified to the power of the flaming sword.

Broken stumps were ripped and burned, and just as Avery leaned over to examine one, he felt the earth shake. He looked up, and saw the giant towering over the trees in the distance. The giant had spotted Avery, and was closing in on him with enormous strides.

With his heart pounding, Avery looked around for a place to hide, and then he saw the fairy goblin standing by his side.

"Thank goodness you're here," he said. "Quick, give me

the last pebble."

"I think you should try the stick this time," said the fairy goblin.

"No, the pebble, quickly! The giant is almost upon us."

"Why are you so intent on the pebble? What's wrong with the stick?"

"But the pebbles work so well!"

"Do they? I wasn't aware of it," said the fairy goblin. "In that case, you must be married to the princess by now."

"Well, no. Not yet," admitted Avery.

"Getting close?" asked the fairy goblin.

Avery said nothing.

"Try the stick," said the fairy goblin.

So Avery took the stick.

"What should I do with it?" he asked.

"I don't care," said the fairy goblin. "It makes no difference to me."

"Should I hit him with it?"

"I don't think he'd feel it. It's not a very big stick."

"Well, then, what should I do with it?"

"I have no idea," said the fairy goblin. "I suppose hitting him with it will be as good as anything else."

The next moment the giant's foot crashed down next to Avery. Avery raised the stick, and hit the giant on the shin. The stick broke, and the giant swung his fiery sword. It hissed through the air, shooting flames as it came. The sword sliced off Avery's head, which rolled along the ground, knocked against a tree with a clunk, and lay still.

* * *

When word reached the palace that Avery had been slain by the giant, there was great sadness. The ladies of the court said it was a shame that such a handsome young man should have had his head cut off.

Even Princess Snowflake was affected by the news. She put aside her diamonds, and tied up her hair with a ribbon of black silk. At lunch she ate only the tiniest morsel of food, and didn't smile during the entire meal. She recovered her spirits by dinner, but when she went to bed that night, a tear fell from her beautiful eyes. It was only a single tear, but who knows what a tear may lead to? No springtime ever came that didn't begin with the melting of the first crystal of ice

After the giant slew Avery, he picked him up, and brought him to his cave, which was carved into the side of a mountain. The giant threw him into a corner, and then left to go knock down more trees.

Avery lay in the giant's cave for three days. His head was too far from his body for him to reach it, and even if he could have reached it, it would have made no difference, because he couldn't move his arms. All he could do was curse the fairy goblin, and wonder what would become of him.

On the third day, the fairy goblin entered the cave, sweating and panting.

"What a climb! You've no idea!"

"Well I've had my head cut off, so don't complain to me."

The fairy goblin inspected Avery's head, paying particular attention to the place where the giant's sword had cut through the neck.

"That's some nice work," he said. "How did it feel?"

"Unpleasant," said Avery. "By the way, thank you so much for the stick. It was a big help."

"Yes, I knew it would be."

"You idiot! The stick was no help at all. It was useless."

"Why do you say that?"

"Because my head's been cut off!"

"Well, pick it up, and let's get going."

The fairy goblin gave Avery's head a kick, and it rolled across the floor of the cave toward his body. Avery found that he could move his arms again, so he reached out to retrieve his head. It was tricky work, because his eyes watched his arms from about a foot away, and he wasn't quite sure which way to move them. It's like trying to cut your hair looking in a mirror. Nothing goes in the right direction.

At last he managed to grab hold of his head, and he placed it on his neck. The world felt a little more normal. Unfortunately, there was nothing to keep his head in place, so he had to hold it up with his hands, which made his shoulders ache.

"Follow me," said the fairy goblin.

He led Avery to the back of the cave, where there was a crack in the wall. The fairy goblin squeezed through the crack, and Avery followed. They found themselves in a narrow corridor of rock, walking along a thin path that sloped downward. The path was long, and after a while Avery's arms became tired, so he took his head off his shoulders, and tucked it under his arm.

"This is a strange way of looking at the world," he said, speaking from the level of his belly. "It makes me feel small and insignificant."

The fairy goblin, who was not quite three feet tall, glared at Avery. But overall, carrying his head under his arm wasn't a bad arrangement. The only difficulty came when he had to squeeze through a part of the cave where the ceiling hung low. Sometimes he misjudged the height of the rock. Fortunately, when this happened, he didn't bang his head, only his shoulders.

The path continued to slope downward, and Avery thought they must have come to the bottom of the giant's mountain, and were now travelling deep inside the earth. The path became wider, and soon it met up with an underground river. The dark water glittered with sparks of phosphorescence that lit the cave, but there were no colors—only shades of gray. The fairy goblin led Avery along the river bank, and everywhere he looked Avery saw the strangest things.

There were gray trees with branches like rubber that waved back and forth in an invisible wind. Outlandish creatures scuttled on the ground in a variety of shapes and sizes. They had gray fur and black eyes. Some were as big as dogs, while others were no larger than a bug. They all looked different, and Avery wondered how many kinds he could count. Then he wondered if they were all the same. When he followed one with his eyes, he saw that it constantly changed shape. No creature was the same for more than a minute at a time.

The creatures ignored Avery, keeping their eyes on the ground. They seemed to be searching for something, but Avery thought that whatever it was, they lost interest in it quickly. They scurried along, then without warning, they darted off in a new direction, making Avery dizzy as he watched them.

"I've never seen a place like this before," he said.

"I should think not," said the fairy goblin. "There aren't many men who can travel back and forth between the worlds of the living and the dead."

"Am I dead then?" asked Avery.

"Of course you're dead," said the fairy goblin. "Your head's been cut off."

"I see what you mean," said Avery.

They left the strange creatures behind them, and traveled deeper into the earth. After a while, Avery heard the splashing of water, and the two travelers climbed down a stairway cut into the rock. When they reached the bottom, Avery saw that the river flowed over the top of the rock, and formed a waterfall about fifteen feet high. The black water became an explosion of sparks as it crashed into the pool below.

"In you go," said the fairy goblin, nudging Avery forward.

"What are you doing?" said Avery. "Cut it out."

There was something about the river that had made Avery nervous from the moment he first saw it. He didn't like the idea of swimming in it.

"Look at you. You're a mess," said the fairy goblin. "If you want me to take you any farther you're going to need to clean yourself up."

The fairy goblin was right. Avery was covered with dirt and blood from his encounter with the giant. But still, he shrank from the eerie water that bubbled and sparked.

"Here, let me help you," said the fairy goblin, giving Avery a sharp push from behind.

Water splashed as Avery fell into the pool. It was freezing. First the water made Avery's skin burn with cold, then his body became numb, but after splashing around for a few minutes, it started to feel refreshing. With careful hands Avery floated his head on the surface of the pool, then rubbed all the dirt and blood from his skin. Next, he decided to try the waterfall. He didn't want any of the water to get into his neck, so he put his head on his shoulders again, and stood on the rocks beneath the cataract.

In an instant, all his senses were wide awake. Avery's vision became perfectly clear, and he realized that he had spent his whole life looking through cloudy eyes. He felt he could see forever.

There was a popping in his ears, and all the sounds around him became not only louder, but easier to understand. He heard patterns in the splashing of the waterfall he hadn't noticed before. The sound of the water crashing down into the pool was a symphony of music.

Avery sneezed, and the air in his lungs shot through his nose. He took a deep breath, and the air rushed back in, accompanied by the cold, clean spray of the waterfall. It had a mineral smell that made Avery feel brisk, and gave him the odd feeling of wanting to do math problems.

The sneeze had been big, and it made Avery realize that his head was once again attached to his body. Just to be sure, he shook it back and forth as fast as he could, like a dog coming in from the rain. Water flew in all directions from his hair, but his head stayed on tight.

He thought it would be fun to climb the rocks and dive down, skimming the surface of the sparkling waterfall, as he plunged into the pool below. But the fairy goblin was becoming impatient, so he got out of the water, shook his body once more, and the two of them resumed their walk through the cave.

Avery's muscles tingled pleasantly, so he stretched out his arms, and said "Ahhh" like someone taking a sip of hot chocolate. It felt good, so he did it a few more times until the fairy goblin told him to please stop.

The path sloped downward again, leading them away from the river. The sparks in the water no longer lit the cave, and it grew dark. The more they walked, the darker it became, and for a long time, neither of them spoke. At last, the darkness and the silence became oppressive, and Avery asked,

"Are we going any place in particular?"

"You are," said the fairy goblin.

"What about you?"

"I'm going back."

"Can I go back?" asked Avery.

"No," said the fairy goblin.

They walked on. The cave became darker and darker, and the silence grew deeper.

"Will I be here long?" asked Avery.

"Oh, yes," said the fairy goblin.

"Forever?"

"Definitely," said the fairy goblin. "Hasn't anyone ever told you what being dead means?"

Avery didn't like the idea of being alone in the dark forever. He wished the fairy goblin would stay with him, at least for a while, until he got used to the darkness. He thought that even the company of Princess Snowflake would be better than being all alone.

At last the path came to an end. Ahead of them rose a great stone blocking the way. There was nowhere left to go.

"This is the place," said the fairy goblin. "Phew, that was a long walk. I hope you appreciate it."

"Thank you for all you've done," said Avery. "I'll miss you."

"I suppose I'll miss you, too," said the fairy goblin, "though I can't imagine why. Here, give me a hand with this rock."

The fairy goblin put his back to the stone in front of them, and began to push. The stone moved, a gap opened, and the cave was flooded with light. Avery hurried to the fairy goblin's side, and soon the two of them had pushed the stone completely out of the way. Avery looked out through the opening.

The view was from a high mountain top, but instead of snow and ice, there was a green meadow bathed in warm sunlight. A young woman was walking across the meadow toward the entrance to the cave.

She came closer, and Avery caught his breath as he saw her face. His first thought was to wonder how Princess Snowflake had gotten here, but then he realized it couldn't be her. Even with all her diamonds and furs, Princess Snowflake had never been as beautiful as the young woman who now entered the cave. She smiled, and Avery recognized her. It was Sophie.

"Sophie!" he gasped. "What happened to you?"

"Didn't anyone tell you?" she said. "I died."

"But you are as beautiful as the dawn."

The young woman blushed.

"That's only because I've loved you for so long, Avery, and now my heart is all I have left. They buried my body in the village churchyard."

"Then my body must still be in the giant's cave," said Avery. "What about my heart, Sophie? How does it look?"

Sophie looked.

"Exactly as I remember it," she said.

Sophie turned to the fairy goblin.

"Thank you for bringing him here."

"It wasn't easy," said the fairy goblin. "He kept insisting on the pebbles. That's why it took so long."

Sophie knelt down, and gave the fairy goblin a kiss. The

fairy goblin blushed to the tips of his ears, and then he was gone.

Sophie stood up, and looked down at her hands.

"I'm sorry I told you to marry Princess Snowflake," she said in a quiet voice.

"That's all right," said Avery. "I never stopped thinking about you, you know."

"I know," she said.

The cave is empty, and the stone door slides closed. Through the narrowing gap of light, two figures can be seen walking hand-in-hand beneath the morning sun. One of them whispers in the other's ear, and they both laugh.

With a breath of air that sounds like a sigh, the door closes shut. The light is hidden, and the stone settles back into place.